I0571854

FATED FOR THE DUKE

ENDURING LEGACY

Christina McKnight

Copyright © 2018 by Christina McKnight
Cover Image by Period Images
Cover Design by Sweet n' Spicy Designs
Vector images used under Creative Commons Attribution License: EezyPremium on Vecteezy

ISBN-13: 978-1-945089-48-0

La Loma Elite Publishing

All rights reserved. No part of this publication may be reproduced, distributed, or transmitted in any form or by any means, including photocopying, recording, or other electronic or mechanical methods, without the prior written permission of the author, except in the case of brief quotations embodied in critical reviews and certain other noncommercial uses permitted by copyright law. For permission requests, write to the author, addressed "Attention: Permissions Coordinator," at the address below.

Christina@christinamcknight.com

DEDICATION

For Marc

PRAISE FOR CHRISTINA MCKNIGHT'S NOVELS

THE THIEF STEALS HER EARL
"When I started reading this book I could not put it down...it caused another book-hangover for me. I wanted to see how things would go when the truth of Judith came out and how Simon was going to handle it...loved it."-*Sissy's Book Review*

"Jude and Cart's story is such a delight! So refreshing to see the hero shy, socially awkward and not super wealthy. I love it...This was definitely one of the best books I've read this summer." -*Reviews from a Thrifty Mom*

FORGOTTEN NO MORE
"This author has made me love historical romance again." -*TwinsieTalk Book Reviews*

HIDDEN NO MORE
"The storyline was really good, the writing was great. So smooth and engaging, I was able to zip right through the story, it flowed so well. I love finding new to me authors and with this wonderfully written story by Ms. McKnight I've found a new historical romance author."-*Bound by Books*

CHRISTMAS EVER MORE
"*Christmas Ever More* was a wonderfully written festive novella full of hope, renewal, love, and new beginnings. If you're a fan of Christina's Lady Forsaken series, this is a must. Even if you aren't caught up, this stands well enough on its own to be a lovely addition to your holiday reading list."-*Literal Addiction*

BOOKS BY CHRISTINA MCKNIGHT

The Undaunted Debutantes Series
The Disappearance of Lady Edith
The Misfortune of Lady Lucianna
The Misadventures of Lady Ophelia
The Season of Lady Chastity
The Desires of Lady Prudence

Lady Archer's Creed Series
Theodora
Georgina
Adeline
Josephine

Craven House Series
The Thief Steals Her Earl
The Mistress Enchants Her Marquis
The Madame Catches Her Duke
The Gambler Wagers Her Baron

A Lady Forsaken Series
Shunned No More
Forgotten No More
Scorned Ever More
Christmas Ever More
Hidden No More

Standalone Titles
The Siege of Lady Aloria
A Kiss at Christmastide
For the Love of a Widow
Earl of St. Seville
The Lady Loves a Scandal
Bound by the Christmastide Moon
Bedded Under the Christmastide Moon
Fated for the Duke

PROLOGUE

Sunderland, England
December 1802

EMILIA, ALONG WITH her three siblings and their *seanmhair*, lowered themselves into the root cellar, taking the long ladder down one rung at a time, their grandmother bringing up the rear. The pungent, heavy aroma of ripening vegetables and her father's treasured wine barrels greeted Emilia much like a warm, familiar embrace.

Each year, for all her life, it had been the same.

Seanmhair Ailis had brought Emilia, Moire, Iain, and Catriona into the musty cellar every year since their births. As they each learned to walk without assistance, the first ladder they had descended led into this dark, dank, windowless room through a trap door in their butler's pantry. And *Seanmhair* demanded they each make the climb unassisted and without a candle to guide them.

It had been a frightening experience when Emilia was younger, but as her siblings were born, and she was charged with minding them, the practice became one of routine and comfort as they lost sight of the importance of the journey. Her mother and father no longer participated and were known to chastise *Seanmhair* for her old-world traditions.

"Come now, me wee ones," *Seanmhair* said, gathering Emilia and her siblings close as she knelt down to look each in the eyes, her knees cracking with the effort. "Do ye ken why we be down here?"

Emilia remained silent, the thick air in the room dampening her short locks as if she stood not in a root cellar, but in a light spring mist.

It was not her place to answer *Seanmhair* Ailis. She'd made the climb down into the root cellar for ten years now. No, on this day, it was Moire, Emilia's youngest sister—aged only five winters—who was to speak.

Seanmhair's crystal blue stare fairly glowed in the dark, cramped space as she took in each child in turn. Though her glare was intense, Emilia saw the faint, green glow hovering about the old woman. Even with *Seanmhair* Ailis's aged and weathered appearance, her drooping cheeks and the creases about her eyes and mouth, Emilia saw it.

Love.

Seanmhair Ailis loved them all very much.

It made this moment all the more imperative. Ailis wasn't attempting to frighten them or cause them any lasting night terrors. No, she was warning them...*preparing* them for a future they may not escape as she had.

Catriona sighed, elbowing Moire to get on

with answering the question.

Moire, named for one of their Scottish ancestors, straightened her shoulders and notched up her chin a degree as she mirrored *Seanmhair's* serious glare and recited what she'd been made to memorize. "We mustn't ever put from mind that we are all special. Our gifts, blessed unto us by our Dalais ancestors, are of great privilege and should not be used for evil. We are descendants of a trio of powerful siblings—Niall, Sorcha, and Caitriona—who gave up their lives to bring each of us into this world." Moire picked at the fraying edge of her pinafore, and Emilia had the nearly overpowering urge to assist her, to speak up and tell their grandmother what she waited to hear.

When Emilia made to do just that, *Seanmhair's* piercing blue eyes swung her way—a warning to remain silent.

As swiftly as the warning glare had turned to Emilia, the elder woman turned back to Moire with an encouraging nod. "Go on, *m'eudail.*"

Moire's lips pulled wide in a smile that had enchanted their entire family since the girl's birth. Emilia's sister loved when their grandmother spoke to them in her native Scottish tongue and called her things like *my darling.* "We are to trust in our gifts. We are to trust in one another. And, above all else, we are to be leery of any person not of Dalais blood."

"Very good, me sweet." Their *seanmhair* pushed to her feet, though even at full height she was little taller than Emilia and Iain. If not for her ailing, stooped body and grey hair, she could easily pass for a child from a distance. Though, up close, her dress, her speech, and her repose were of a different time. "Now, tell me, me bairns, what know ye of this moment?"

Iain grunted and crossed his arms. "I despise this part."

"What have I told ye, lad?" *Seanmhair* snapped, placing her crooked, knotty hand on Iain's shoulder.

Emilia's brother stared at his scuffed boots as he transferred his weight from one foot to the other. "That the gifts chose us, and there is naught we can say about it. But it still isn't fair, not one little bit that Em, Moire, and Cat were chosen, and I am nothing...barely a Noble at all."

"Me darling lad." Their grandmother's tone softened, and she stepped until she faced Iain, her fingers lifting his chin until he stared directly at her. "Ye were blessed with beauty, wealth, and title. The luck born of a male heir. Ye canna expect to have everything."

Iain pulled away from his *seanmhair*. "I'd rather have the mark and a gift like my great-great-great-great-grandfather, Lochlan."

"You know males of the Dalais bloodline have not been blessed with the mark for many decades," Cat chimed in. "Even Father was given no gift, and he is strong, and brave, and courageous."

"And a bore," Iain mumbled.

Moire giggled at her brother's proclamation.

Even Emilia could not suppress a grin, though she did not dare laugh at such a solemn time.

"Moire," the older woman prodded, giving the girl's long, fiery red plait a gentle tug. "What do ye see?"

The girl gulped, her shoulders quaking ever so slightly. "I'd rather Cat or Em speak first."

"Verra well." *Seanmhair* turned to Emilia, the first grandchild born with the legacy mark on her left hip. A simple triangle, but a gift their family feared would not be bestowed upon the Noble family again. "What do ye see, me wee lass?"

It hadn't been until Emilia began to speak that her family had discovered her special gift. She could see the energy of those around her with the enhanced ability to recognize when another was lying. With her grandmother's help, Emilia had worked to understand what each color and hazy glow meant.

"I see…" Her words trailed off as a dark, brownish-yellow surrounded the woman. Her *seanmhair* was fatigued, yet other colors pushed through as Emilia scrutinized her grandmother. "Violet and gold show you are imparting great wisdom. And green, as always, envelops you."

Love. Kindness. Caring.

Seanmhair Ailis nodded curtly and turned to Cat. "And ye, me wee kitten?"

Cat closed her eyes, her brow pulling low with her effort. Catriona had been the most impacted by her gift: the ability to connect with another's emotional state. With great work, their grandmother had taught Cat how to harness her gift and not allow it to overwhelm her. For a period, Cat had been utterly weighed down by the burdens of those around her, whether it be someone in their family or even the villagers they passed in town.

Emilia watched as Cat worried her bottom lip until a tiny bead of blood marred her perfect flesh.

If Emilia had been given a choice, she would have taken all three gifts unto herself, if only to save her two sisters from the oppressive nature of their abilities.

The gift of sight. The gift of empathy. And the gift to read another's energy force.

Seanmhair Ailis had been the only one of her

siblings chosen, though she'd been given thrice the gifts, and the completed legacy mark: three overlaid triangles. If one combined Emilia's, Cat's, and Moire's marks, it would mirror the birthmark on their grandmother's chest, just below her collarbone.

"I see you are frantic, *Seanmhair*. There is an urgency surrounding you I do not understand." Cat glanced at Moire, begging her to help, but her younger sister averted her gaze.

"Moire?" Emilia questioned.

"*Seanmhair* is not long for this world," Moire whispered before a cry escaped her. "*Seanmhair* Ailis, I wish to go back above. I do not want to do this any longer. My vision…it is cruel, and I will not allow it to come true."

"Tsk-tsk." Their grandmother shook her head but not in sorrow. "Me dearest, Moire. Ye may see the future, but ye can do naught to change it. It not be the way of things. Not at all."

Iain pushed back into the circle Emilia, Moire, Cat, and their *seanmhair* had created without them realizing it.

"Tell us Moire is wrong," Iain demanded. "She is but a baby and cannot know what she says." He looked to his eldest sister for something—perhaps guidance—and Emilia longed to reassure him of their future. Alas, she could not.

Despite their shared eye color and appearances, it was Emilia who had hair of the palest blond, nearly white in the sun, which set her apart from her siblings and even her *seanmhair*.

At eight, Emilia's younger brother, Iain, was a boy surrounded by strong women, their Scottish heritage, pale skin, and fiery hair only making their spirit more apparent. While he shared the family's coloring as well as their piercing blue eyes, he was more like their father—a boy willing to allow the women in his family to lead.

Perhaps the boy had more spirit then they'd given him credit for.

Iain turned to Emilia, looking for an ally. "Em, tell them this is absurd. *Seanmhair* is well and will be going nowhere. Not for a long, long time. We need her. You have yet to master your gift, and Moire…can we trust her visions?"

Emilia knew Moire spoke only the truth. Sometimes, her gift was also a curse, just as it was for Catriona and Moire.

"Moire be correct, wee ones." *Seanmhair* pulled all four children close, and Emilia accepted her embrace, pushing farther into her hold as if them all banding together and never letting go could stop her grandmother's encroaching fate. "I be gone soon enough, and the group of ye shall move on from Dalais Forge—Edinburgh, Bath, and London. The world is yours to explore. But ye must stay close. Depend on each other. Listen to one another."

"Yes, *Seanmhair* Ailis," they spoke in unison, each bowing their heads.

Emilia's chest ached at the thought of living even a moment without her grandmother near. She wanted to cry, to wail about the unfairness of it all, to stomp her foot and demand it not come to pass.

Alas, her bout of anger and sadness would do naught to change their future.

"Now, me wee lasses, remember…one day a friend, and the next a foe. Ye need to rely on each other, trust in only each other. I won't be here to protect ye much longer."

"What of me?" Iain demanded, his tone

rising in panic.

"Ye, lad, will listen to ye sisters." Her stern words had Iain swallowing any retort he may have had. "These three care for ye, Iain. Even when ye think ye know best, ye don't."

Emilia thought her *seanmhair* was being too harsh and severe with Iain.

But, again, she kept quiet.

"It is getting late, and me bones are aching." *Seanmhair* Ailis swept her long, grey hair back over her shoulder and fixed each of them with one last stare. "Ye all need to find ye beds. Off with the lot of ye."

Iain was the first to turn and scurry up the ladder into the butler's pantry. His footsteps could be heard above as he fled. Cat was far more hesitant in her departure, her steps slow as she climbed into the light from above and waited for her sisters to follow. Finally, Emilia took hold of the lower rung and hoisted herself up as her *seanmhair* spoke in a hushed voice to Moire. Her words of caution drifted up to Emilia...

"Moire, me wee darling, ye canna speak of that to ye sister. The future be what it is, with or without ye meddling..."

Emilia climbed ever higher until she reached the top, Catriona's soft cries falling from above, even though her *seanmhair's* words tempted Emilia back down to the cellar. Despite her tears, Cat held her hand out to help Emilia out.

Behind them, they listened to the scraping of Moire's half-boots as she too climbed up the ladder. The day seemed final: the end of a long-held, sacred tradition.

Emilia did not want to move away from Dalais Forge, nor be without her *seanmhair*.

CHAPTER 1

Epsom, England
September 1811

FELIX HUNTAR, THE Duke of Kintore, leaned against the railing separating him and the gathered crowd from the thoroughbreds, Arabian, and Quarter horses that ran at Epsom Downs Racetrack. While the assembled spectators were swathed in a stupor of anticipation and excitement, Felix could list no less than fifteen important tasks he *should* be attending to rather than wasting his day two hours from London proper. The races were no higher on his priority list than selecting fish at Spitalfields Market, walking the promenade at Hyde Park, or...he shuddered at the thought, attending a musicale recital brimming with boisterous mums seeking to ensnare a wealthy, titled husband for their vapid, uninspired daughters.

Doing his utmost to appear at ease and without any genuine concerns in the world other than the anticipated victor in the race about to start, Felix surveyed the men and several women pressing toward the railing behind him until he spotted his uncle, the Earl of Abernathy. The elder gentleman slung his arm around a young man of no more than seventeen as they moved down the rail to secure a better view of the race.

Felix didn't recognize the other man. His fiery red hair was cut and combed to perfection, and he had skin so pale he would surely burn, even in the overcast September warmth. Tall and lanky, the lad was not his uncle's normal crony, far from it, actually, though his jacket and breeches were of excellent quality.

That fact alone had Felix studying the pair closer.

When his uncle's butler had sent word to Kintore Manor that morning, Felix had had half a mind to ignore the missive. Playing nursemaid to an aging man had grown old and tiresome years before; however, if things went awry, it was Felix who'd be called upon to repair the damage.

And Felix would be fooling himself if he did not accept at least part of the blame for his uncle's current circumstances.

The crowd let loose a gasp as the jockeys were signaled to start their race.

Felix kept a close watch on his uncle. Lord Abernathy had been Felix's guardian until he reached his majority and inherited his father's dukedom. Felix glanced past his uncle and the young man to see his driver, Jameson, lounging close to the rail farther down.

Felix and his driver had been through this many times over the years, though they were usually in a tavern or down close to the docks.

Felix was unwed and without children, yet he mused having his uncle around must be akin to having at least a dozen offspring.

Nodding at Jameson, Felix turned to watch the final lap of the race as several horses vied for position. The dust kicked up from their thundering hooves coated the onlookers in a thick layer of grime. No one seemed to mind as all eyes followed the lead horse. The entire gathering was in a trance-like state. In fact, they inched forward as the horses progressed around the track.

Felix had never understood the allure of gambling or the enthusiasm surrounding horse racing.

Perhaps because he'd been raised by his uncle, Abner Key, who'd spent just as much time deep in his cups as he did placing misguided and outright foolish wagers in gaming hells at the docks and at the races.

It hadn't been until he attended Eton Felix had realized that not all men drank themselves into a stupor each night before bed. Not all gentlemen spent the better part of their lives slinking from one hovel to another, night after never-ending night on a mission to spend their last shilling on liquor, women, and gaming.

Felix shook his head, refocusing his attention on Abner where he swayed from side to side, the young man still pulled close as they cheered and jeered from their spot near the rail.

"Go! Go! Go!" the crowd shouted as three horses approached the finish line, neck and neck.

The anticipatory air was in no way contagious for Felix.

As the horses crossed the line, some in the crowd cheered, while others shouted in anger.

His uncle, as was typical, was part of the latter group.

Another lost bet.

Felix only hoped the sum was not too large. The Abernathy earldom was essentially destitute, driven into ruin by Abner's need to gamble, drink, and carouse on an endless loop.

Felix started for the pair as Abner shoved the younger man, who stumbled back, knocking into a matronly lady and causing her fan and parasol to sail through the air. Jameson quickly collected the articles and returned them to the woman, who fled toward the refreshments with two other ladies in tow.

Felix moved swiftly through the crowd toward his uncle as he advanced on the man, no longer swaying on unsteady feet.

Felix supposed a significant loss for his uncle was a sobering experience.

Jameson had nearly reached the red-haired man, and Felix grew closer to his uncle just as Abner pulled back his fist and pummeled the man he'd arrived with in the face. The redhead's nose exploded with a gush of red that closely matched his locks as it streamed down his face to stain his white linen shirt.

Shocked, the man stumbled backwards again, colliding with Jameson as the driver attempted to steady the lad.

Felix leapt between the two men as his uncle advanced again.

"What in the hell is going on here, Uncle?" Felix looked between Abner and his associate, realizing he was little more than a boy, despite his height and presence at Epsom Downs.

He hated the need to scold his uncle as if he were a child. He despised the fact that Abner knew his nephew would always come to his rescue and right his wrongs. He loathed the fact that his parents had passed away and left him in the scoundrel's care for so many years.

Felix took a calming breath as the gawking crowd began to dissipate, the action ending as quickly as it had begun. The onlookers drifted away from the racetrack to collect their winnings and begin their two-hour carriage ride back to town.

Which left Felix, Jameson, Abner, and the young man, the bruise on his nose already turning purple as the blood halted.

What an utter disaster.

"What is the meaning of all this?" Felix hissed, attempting to keep their altercation from those surrounding them.

Abner tore his seething stare from the lad long enough to pin his nephew with a hard glare. "Do enlighten me as to why *you* are here? I do not need you meddling in my affairs."

"I witnessed quite the opposite just now," Felix retorted before clamping his mouth shut. The last thing he needed was his uncle baiting him into an argument before so many members of the *ton*.

"I...should...be going," the lad mumbled, attempting to pull away from Jameson, who only held him tighter.

Felix glared between Abner and the boy, silently waiting for either man to explain themselves.

"As it happens, I have all day, gentlemen." Felix crossed his arms, his shoulders relaxing somewhat now that the young man was no longer in danger of another assault.

The other man shifted from foot to foot. "I...well...Lord Aber—"

"I will tell *you* what is what," Abner cut the

boy off. "This—this—*swindler*...he said he knew the winning horse." His uncle's brown eyes narrowed on the young man. "So I bet all my coin and then some, only to have it all lost."

It was precisely what Felix should have expected from Abner. "This man, like any other, can no more know the winning horse as he can the turn of a card."

"Not true. The boy has a gift. I have witnessed it on many occasions." Abner rounded on the red-haired man, poking his finger into his bloodied shirt. "Yet now, when the stakes are high, you think to cheat me? I won't stand for it. I won't."

The scene was verging on comical. If only Abner had had the foresight to stomp his foot like a petulant child being denied a second sweet. Unfortunately, Felix knew how swiftly his uncle's moods swung and kept any hint of amusement from his face.

"Uncle, I think it is time you return home." Felix nodded to Jameson over Abner's shoulder. "Jameson will see you to your coach, and I will see your...friend home safely." And make the appropriate apologies to his family for his state of injury.

This time, Abner did stomp his foot. "You cannot order me about. I am your guardian, not the other way around. You will show me the respect bestowed upon me by my sister."

"*Were*," Felix replied, the ease he'd regained once again leaving his shoulders.

"What was that?" Abner sidestepped Jameson as the servant moved forward to guide him toward the waiting carriages.

"I said were, Uncle. You *were* my guardian. However, I reached my majority years ago."

Felix recognized the fire lighting within his

uncle.

"After all I've given you...all I gave *up* for you!" Abner seethed. "My estate suffered because I was tending to you, my orphaned nephew. I never wed because I was seeing to your upbringing and education. I put my future on hold because I was tasked with the responsibility of...*you*."

Felix remained silent, listening to the tirade he'd heard at least a hundred times over the last several years. What his uncle failed to mention was that he was already a confirmed scoundrel when he was called upon to care for Felix; already a known gambler and drunkard. Lord Abernathy's estate was destitute long before Felix's mother and father had passed away. If anything, Abner had been able to live a lavish lifestyle *because* he'd been charged with caring for his nephew.

"The boy has a gift. Can see the future, he claims." Abner started for the young man once more, but Felix's look halted him in his tracks. "Do not look at me as if I am a loon. He's known the winner nearly half a dozen times so far. We've made a bloody fortune. But now, it is all gone—"

"Enough." Felix slashed his hand through the air between himself and his uncle, the young man recoiling in terror. "Uncle, you will go home to Berkeley Square. I will see your friend home and meet you there afterwards." Felix met his driver's controlled stare. "Please, see my uncle to his carriage, Jameson."

When Jameson attempted to grasp Abner's shoulder, his uncle brushed off the hold and stomped off toward his waiting coach, which was parked next to Felix's conveyance.

"I—I—I—can find my way home," the

young man stumbled over his words.

"I think not," Felix mused, taking in the redhead's state. "Your shirt is ruined, and I doubt you have the coin for the return trip to London. You arrived in Lord Abernathy's coach, did you not?"

"Y-y-y-yes."

Felix wondered how his uncle and the boy had come to know one another. He was not Abner's usual comrade in any way. The earl was known to cozy up to other drunkards and gamblers or attach himself to gentlemen with deep pockets who funded his wagers.

"Your name?" Felix inquired.

"Iain." The young man stared down at his scuffed boots coated in dust and muck from the track. "Iain Noble." He cleared his throat and lifted his chin. "Lord Strathmore."

"I am Felix, Duke of Kintore." Felix started for the coaches, and the lad fell into step with him. "If you will allow me, I would like to see you home."

"I suppose," Iain mumbled.

"Wonderful. What is your direction?" Felix nodded at Jameson when he opened the carriage door.

With a gesture, Felix indicated that Iain should alight before him. The last thing he needed was the lad taking off if Felix entered the coach first.

But Iain made no other protests as he took the rear-facing seat. "Cavendish Square, number eight. I live with my...family."

"Very good." Felix rapped his knuckles on the side of the coach, and Jameson closed the door before climbing up onto his perch. The conveyance ambled into motion, making its way through the rutted coach area to the road leading back into town. "I would like to make amends for my uncle's deplorable behavior."

"That is not necessary, Your Grace."

Iain—Lord Strathmore, as it were—scrubbed his hand where the blood from his nose had dried.

"I must disagree with you," Felix said, shaking his head.

"I deserved the jab." Iain moved on from his hand to inspect his shirt.

"No one deserves a blow like that, especially in such a public place." When the young man said nothing in return, Felix pulled back the cloth covering his window and watched as the landscape passed by.

Felix wanted to ask why Iain had taken up with the likes of the Earl of Abernathy, yet it was not his business to know the lad's reasons.

Abner...Abner was a different concern.

Felix had, in no way, finished handling the situation with his uncle. Assaulting a man at the track...it was uncalled for and ungentlemanly, no matter how much coin Abner had lost on the race. Ladies had been present, for God's sake.

Felix reclined in his seat, content to remain quiet on the remainder of their journey back to London. Before long, Iain dozed off across from him, his head lolling to one side with the gentle sway of the carriage.

Iain's nose was swelling and would likely bruise more from the blow, but Felix suspected the injury would be gone, and his face healed in a week's time. However, Iain's fair complexion meant the bruise would be all the more noticeable until it faded.

Felix welcomed the distraction of seeing Iain home, for it gave his temper time to cool before he confronted Abner. He'd known for some time that things could not continue as they had thus far: Abner finding trouble at every turn, and Felix fixing it out of an unrelenting sense of guilt and obligation to the man.

For the longest time, he'd wondered why his father—and his mother—had put him in his uncle's care. But, recently, Felix had begun to suspect that his parents hadn't actually intended for Abner to care for Felix, but for Felix to watch over Abner.

Would his uncle have ceased drinking, wed a proper lady, and started a family had he not been charged with Felix's upbringing? There was no way to know the trajectory of their lives had things not transpired as they had.

The ache in Felix's chest grew, bringing the familiar tightness across his shoulders as he attempted to block out thoughts of the past. There was no changing what had happened, nor did Felix want to.

He was the man he was because of it all.

Tilting back his head, he stared at the ceiling of the coach. As the time passed, he recognized the motion of the conveyance changing as they traveled from the country roads to the cobbled streets of town and slowed their speed.

Before long, the coach came to a halt, and Jameson jumped from his post and opened the carriage door.

Leaning forward, Felix was afforded a view of number 8, Cavendish Square. Well-maintained, if not the grandest of London townhouses. White with black trim and five steps leading to red double doors. The carriage was parked on the street, as there was no drive leading to the home, nor shrubs of any sort planted in boxes out front.

Felix cleared his throat. "We have arrived."

Iain startled awake, glancing toward Felix before his stare darted around the enclosed coach and out the open door to his townhouse. If it were possible for the man to pale further, he did.

"Shall we?" Felix gestured to the open door.

"I can see myself in, Your Grace." Could it be that the young man was more terrified of Felix accompanying him to his door than he'd been while faced with Abner's fist? "I thank you for the ride."

The last thing Felix needed was the boy's family seeking retribution for the altercation between Abner and Iain. "I will walk with you."

It would also do well for Felix to warn the boy's father about the type of men his son was keeping company with.

When Iain made no move, Felix hopped from the coach and started for the door where Jameson was standing, waiting for his cue to knock.

Felix waved his driver away back to his place by the coach. Another occurrence he didn't relish was pomp and circumstance getting in the way of him making amends with Iain's father. By the time Felix had taken the steps up to the door, Iain was behind him.

Lifting the metal knocker, Felix rapped it three times for good measure and, instantly, he heard movement from within. Had Iain's family noticed the lad's absence? Had they been looking for him?

The door swung open, and Felix's stare did not meet that of a butler or even the lord of the house but the sapphire blue stare of a petite woman, her hair so fair it was nearly white.

Any apology or greeting he'd prepared on their journey back to London fled him.

He searched his mind but could only come

up with words such as *sprite, pixie,* and *utterly captivating.*

Despite her narrowing stare, the woman before him was…

"May I help you?" Her rich, melodic tone fit her perfectly. He did not believe in fairies, nor fables, but if ever pixies frolicked in the English countryside, this woman would be their muse. "Sir?"

The seconds passed slowly as Felix remained frozen, unable to speak, think, or move.

Felix realized he was holding his breath and exhaled in a whoosh.

The woman looked him up and down with an intensity that suited her despite her whimsical appearance.

"I am the Duke of Kintore—"

Before he could properly introduce himself, the woman's eyes traveled past him and landed on Iain.

MOIRE RECLINED WITH a soft smile as her vision cleared once more, bringing her back to her family's sitting room, her needlepoint still clutched in her hands as the prick of pain in her thumb had her setting it aside.

A single droplet of blood marred the tip of her thumb.

Far less than her brother had been subjected to.

An unfortunate circumstance that was necessary to see the future proceed according to her visions. Certainly, Iain would forgive her for misleading him in such a cruel manner once everything with Emilia and her future was assured.

She glanced toward the open door her sister had departed through only a few short minutes before.

"What are you up to, dear sister?"

Moire glanced toward Catriona where she sat, reading a book close to the window overlooking the garden behind their family townhouse. She did not even avert her stare from the pages as she spoke.

"You are feeling rather pleased with yourself, and I will know why," Catriona prodded.

She was rather pleased with herself, as it were; however, her sister would not pry the reason from her. At least, not yet. There was still much to her vision, and she would not have her sister running to Emilia and ruining everything.

"…and why would you bid Em see to the door? If Father caught her greeting guests he would be appalled."

"Fear not, Mother and Father shall not return from their afternoon at the park for another hour or so," she reassured Catriona.

Her sister closed her book with a thud and swung her legs off the window ledge. "I do not like the look you have in your eyes. Do not think I will not go to Mum and speak of this."

Moire only smiled at Catriona.

It was too late. Yes, far too late to stop things now.

They were already in motion…

CHAPTER 2

LADY EMILIA NOBLE drew in a deep breath at the sight of her brother, his shirt bloodied, and his nose enflamed and turning an awful shade of purple. Grime clung to his ruffled hair as a dusty, hazy pink glow surrounded him, hovering about his person but not directly connected to him.

What foolishness had Iain embroiled himself in now? She did not recognize the man with him. At least Iain hadn't thought it comical to release the neighbor's horse again.

"As I was saying, I am the Duke of Kintore." The man—lord—taking up most of her doorway bowed stiffly, and Emilia noted how Iain slid farther behind him as if attempting to keep his aura hidden from her. "I thought it best I return Lord Strathmore to his home—"

Emilia looked back at the stranger. Average height for a man. Not overly tall, nor was he stout in any way. He appeared every bit the London lord she'd become accustomed to since moving to town, except there was something peculiar about this duke. And it had naught to do with his aura. His dark hair slipped over one eye, and he shook his head, the lock returning to its place as if the offending strand had been duly chastised. His eyes were a rich, cocoa brown, nearly as dark as his hair. His tanned skin did little to hide the smudged patches under his eyes, however. Emilia couldn't help wondering if the dark circles hinted at a lack of sleep or perhaps another, far more burdening hardship.

Was this why Moire had instructed her to answer the door before Edwin, their butler, scurried into the foyer?

The brooding duke stepped to the side, allowing Emilia a clear view of Iain and his damaged face, but her eyes lingered on the stranger. Faint remnants of vivid red clung to his aura—anger. In quick order, a pale blue blossomed, with hints of...shimmering pink. Compassion, overridden by...something else.

For not the first time since losing her *seanmhair*, Emilia wished the woman were still with them. There was so much she'd yet to learn about her gift. Namely, what this glistening pink color meant. The pale blue was one she knew well as it surrounded her sister, Catriona, nearly constantly as the girl felt the emotions of others so intensely that it sometimes brought her to her knees.

Emilia silently scolded herself and focused on Iain once more, pushing past the duke to her brother. As she placed her hand on his bruising face, her brother hissed and pulled back as if she'd harmed him. His pale skin was heated from the injury.

Glancing up and down the square, Emilia ushered Iain into the house.

"Do come in, Your Grace," she called over her shoulder. "It will not do to have the neighbors gossiping over my brother." There was little doubt the lady of the manor in one of the abutting townhouses had an ample view of Emilia's front stoop from her front salon.

The duke had the good sense to close the door behind him.

"May I be so bold as to request an audience with Lord Strathmore's father?" the man asked.

"He is not in residence at the moment," Emilia said, scrutinizing Iain's nose. "Did you do this to him?"

Silently, Emilia followed the question with another: *What did Iain do to deserve the pummeling?*

The stranger gasped at her voiced inquiry as if affronted. "Heavens, no."

Emilia took in his aura of honesty. "Then I thank you for seeing him home. I am Lady Emilia Noble, Iain's elder sister. I will see to his injuries."

The man needed to depart before her parents arrived home from Hyde Park, and Emilia needed time to figure out what trouble Iain had gotten himself into, and what needed to be done to see it behind them.

"I will wait for them to return if that pleases you, my lady."

Her stare darted back to the duke where her words almost—*almost*—stuck in her throat. "It very much does not please me, Your Grace."

Though she was angry with Iain and uneasy at having the stranger in their home, Emilia couldn't help but stare at the duke. Despite their time in London, and the many balls she'd attended since her introduction, she'd never laid eyes on the man nor heard the lord's name spoken in powder rooms or whispered behind raised fans. Perhaps he was already wedded and favored time with his family over social engagements.

"Emilia, I—"

At Iain's muttering, Emilia turned her piercing glare on him. She knew exactly how her sapphire blue eyes sizzled when she offered her hard stare. She'd practiced it for years in her bedchamber looking glass. A bright green aura spoke of Iain's dishonesty, though he'd yet to give his accounting of what had transpired when she and her sisters hadn't even noticed he'd left the house.

There was little doubt he planned to deceive her.

"If I may—" the duke started again, his poise sending a shock of annoyance through her. "I stumbled upon your brother at Epsom Downs Racetrack—"

"Epsom?" Emilia asked. "That is south of town, is it not?"

Since leaving Dalais Forge after their *seanmhair's* passing, they'd lived in Edinburgh, Manchester, Bath, and had finally settled in London. However, her family generally never traveled so far south.

"Yes, my lady. And please know I do not relish returning the boy in such a condition. I am not directly the cause of your brother's injuries, but I am afraid I must take a bit of the responsibility." Everything about Kintore spoke to his honesty. "I stumbled upon Iain hanging about the track with my uncle, Lord Abernathy."

"I am confused how that led to his bloodied shirt and swollen face." Emilia's chest tightened.

"It would appear that he and my uncle placed a wager on a horse—and lost."

"Iain?" she hissed. "Is this true?"

Before her brother could respond, the duke continued, "My uncle is under the impression that Lord Strathmore, Iain, can see the future. Apparently, they have been placing wagers for some time in that vein. However, today, they were not so fortunate."

Emilia glanced back at Iain, who was doing his utmost to shrink into the background, waiting for his chance to scurry off and hide. The green of his aura had faded to grey. He felt trapped.

She caught hold of herself before she scolded Iain and begged the tension in her shoulders to ease as she addressed the duke. "See the future? I'm sure it's clear how preposterous that is"—namely because Emilia was well aware Iain had no gift of premonition—"and, frankly, I wonder about Lord Abernathy's mental capabilities if he was lured into such a reverie."

For the first time, Emilia was thankful she could not ascertain her own haze of dishonesty.

She gave a short, forced laugh in an attempt to lighten the heavy mood that had fallen upon the foyer.

Kintore's narrowed stare told her he did not fully believe her. He turned back toward Iain and seemed to scrutinize him, his intense stare starting at her brother's auburn locks and drifting down to his scuffed boots before he turned back to Emilia as if he'd found some proof of what he was searching for.

Could he actually believe that Iain possessed the gift to foretell the future?

"I thank you for pointing out my uncle's folly, Lady Emilia," Kintore said, a slight smile pulling at his lips. A bit of the heaviness that had surrounded the duke lifted as he chuckled. "Abner was not gifted with the good sense to know when something does not resonate as plausible."

"Well, as we can both see, my brother has made some dubious decisions with regards to Lord Abernathy, as well." Her fear at her family's gifts being discovered receded.

The duke reached into his jacket pocket and retrieved his card. "Lady Emilia"—he held out the card to her—"if there is anything Lord Strathmore needs, or if your parents wish to speak about this matter further, my directions are on my card."

Emilia accepted the embossed rectangle, glancing down to see that the duke's townhouse was in Berkeley Square.

"Thank you, Your Grace." Emilia turned the card over in her fingers.

With a low bow and a final glance in Iain's direction, the Duke of Kintore pivoted toward the front door, pausing as if waiting for the door to magically open before him. When it did not, and Edwin—bless the servant—did not hurry into the room, the duke grasped the latch and let himself out, closing the door in his wake.

Leaving Iain and Emilia alone.

"Em, let me—"

"No." Emilia faced her brother, her skirts flaring around her ankles at the sudden movement.

As if on cue, Moire and Catriona skidded into the foyer, Edwin quick behind them as if he'd only just heard the front door close. Catriona immediately hurried to Iain, her expression solemn, and Edwin stepped up to the pair with a damp cloth at the ready.

How had the servant known that Iain would need tending?

Emilia noted Moire hadn't fully entered the foyer from the hall, and had, in fact, slunk back toward the sitting room.

Before Emilia could speak on the matter, Iain spotted their youngest sibling and pushed away Cat's tending and the butler's offered cloth.

Iain's skin flamed red, and Moire squealed, her eyes rounding. She grasped her skirts and took off at a run back down the hallway in the direction she and Cat had come from.

"Moire!" Iain shouted, stomping after her. "You did this on purpose."

"Iain, stop," Cat called, following the pair. "You will injure yourself further."

Emilia's temper flared. She was suddenly thankful that the duke had departed before Moire and Cat reached the foyer. But, then again, she was now certain her youngest sibling had planned it all, even bidding Edwin to be otherwise engaged and unable to attend to his duties with regards to their guest.

Her parents would return any moment from the park, and if they discovered Moire had been using her gift...and Iain had lied about *having* a gift...they would never hear the end of their father's lecture. Calum Noble, the Marquess of Eglinton, knew naught what possessing the legacy gift meant as he'd been born without the mark.

Seanmhair had proclaimed Emilia's father unworthy of the mark until their family had been gifted with a complete trio: Emilia, Catriona, and Moire. Their overlapping birthmarks completed the talisman of their lineage.

"My lady?" Edwin inquired.

She turned to see the butler still clutching the

cloth he'd brought in to cleanse Iain's face. "Edwin, thank you" — she took the cloth — "I will see to Iain."

With a nod of thanks for the butler, Emilia started after her siblings.

It might serve them all right if she told her parents everything and allowed their father to handle the situation. As swiftly as that thought came, however, she dispelled it. *Seanmhair* was adamant that Emilia, Moire, and Cat always be at one another's side — and look after Iain at the same time. In the years since her grandmother's passing, Emilia and her siblings had maintained the close bond they'd developed in their childhood at Dalais Forge.

Even where the Marquess and Marchioness of Eglinton were concerned, Emilia and their siblings stood together.

The door to the sitting room stood wide, and Emilia spied Iain glaring at Moire as Cat attempted to pull him away.

"Look what you have done," Iain seethed. "There is no way I can—"

Emilia stepped into the room and slammed the door shut, silencing Iain and gaining the notice of Catriona and Moire, their fiery red heads both turning toward her.

"What is the meaning of this? I will have your answer immediately," Emilia hissed. Yelling at them would garner her nothing, though explaining the dire implications of their situation might gain her some truth. "Tell me you did not pose as a seer to win coin at the races."

When Iain opened his mouth, and the space around him flared green once more, Emilia held up her hand. She needed to discover exactly how many people her brother had attempted to fool.

"Do not think to lie to me, dear brother. The duke has departed, and it is only us."

"I wasn't doing it for the winnings," Iain said.

"You think that makes it better? Do you presume that excuses your behavior?" Emilia demanded, throwing her hands wide. She realized she still held the duke's card. "What did *Seanmhair* Ailis teach us?"

"A friend can swiftly turn to foe," Moire and Cat recited in unison.

"Lord Abernathy is not a friend," Iain scoffed.

"And yet you spoke of our family secrets?" Emilia could not fathom what had come over her brother. "And now, his nephew, an utter stranger knows."

"I said I had the gift, I said nothing of Moire or Cat—or you, Em." Iain pivoted and sank to the lounge, his head falling into his hands. "And now…now I owe Abner and the bookmaker at The Howling Owl. All because of you."

Iain held Moire's blue stare with his own.

"What have you to do with this, Moire?" Emilia asked.

"Not much…" Her youngest sibling glanced toward her discarded needlepoint.

How had they, only a short time before, been enjoying an afternoon of societally approved female pastimes, and now Emilia feared her entire family could be hunted down at any moment?

"Iain asked me to speak on the future…it was only supposed to be a grand lark." Moire worried her hands before her, and Emilia knew she was at least a bit contrite. "No one was supposed to be harmed."

"And now I have a plum busted nose and

am indebted to Lord Abernathy." Iain ran his hands through his hair, tugging at the ends in frustration. "And that speaks nothing of how much I owe Harris at The Howling Owl, though I can only assume it is a staggering sum. What if Lord Abernathy tells others of my gift?"

"You have no gift." This time, it was Cat and Emilia who spoke at the same time.

Cat slumped onto the window seat, and Emilia feared the overwhelming emotions from her three siblings would be more than Cat could handle.

"It was only supposed to be a spot of fun," Moire countered. "You never said you were wagering any significant amount."

"It wasn't like that at first, but as my horse kept winning, so did Abernathy push for larger bets." Iain sighed, lifting his head and meeting Emilia's stunned stare. "Em, I can fix this. I will figure out how to repay the bookmaker and satisfy Lord Abernathy. I may not possess the gifts the trio of you have, but I have sense enough to mend this."

Pain spiked in the palm of her hand, and Emilia realized she had balled her hand into a fist, the duke's calling card cutting into her palm.

"No, you have done quite enough, Iain," she said, taking in her brother's reticent air. He was regretful—and she was sorry, as well. Emilia released her fist and read the name on the card.

The Sixth Duke of Kintore, Felix Huntar.

If she were not also irritated at Moire, she would ask her sister if the duke's name, Huntar, was meant as a foreshadowing of what was to come.

Friend to foe.

Emilia could not deny that her blood thrummed through her veins with a bit more intensity at the thought of seeing the brooding, dark-haired stranger again.

Instead, she stiffened her shoulders and stared at each of her siblings in turn, finally fixing her gaze on Iain. "I will handle this. Until then, the trio of you is to remain silent on this matter." When they all nodded, she continued, "And for all that is sacred, do not seek out any more trouble."

CHAPTER 3

FELIX HAD EXPECTED Iain's father, Lord Eglinton, to call on him the previous day—or at least send word demanding Felix or his uncle make retribution for the young man's injuries. However, when Felix had finally sought his private chambers during the wee hours of the morning, he'd heard nothing from the marquess.

Which had made it all the more surprising when Percy, Felix's valet, had entered his chambers while Felix was seeing to his dress with word that Felix had a visitor.

A female visitor.

A *young*, female visitor.

The first image that sprang to mind was that of a petite lady with short locks as fair as her pale skin. It hadn't escaped Felix's notice that she was light and soft where he was dark and hard-edged. Certainly, their upbringing had much to do with the differences between them.

His boots echoed in the deserted corridor as he made his way to the blue salon. The room had been his mother's favorite in the entire townhouse, besides when she escaped the indoors for the openness of the gardens. However, the room overlooked the landscaped area behind Kintore Manor.

Before long, Felix found himself in the hall outside the treasured room, and he halted.

Lady Emilia Noble awaited him within.

The door stood ajar, and he spotted her standing close to the window, her gloved hands clenched before her, and her brow pulled low, her mouth moving as if she spoke to someone though no sound escaped her. Nothing about her was the light and airy pixie he'd met the day before. An unseen burden had settled on her, making her shoulders fall forward slightly.

"Has something happened to Lord Strathmore?" he asked as he entered the room, not bothering to keep the worry from his tone or issue a proper greeting to his guest.

Her chin lifted, and her narrowed stare met his before her eyes widened. He'd startled her, and for that, Felix was sorry.

"No—no—no," she stuttered, shaking her head. "He is as well as can be expected after receiving a jab to the face."

The tension that had raced through him at the sight of her in his salon eased ever so slightly. "Why have you come to Kintore Manor?"

She glanced over his shoulder. "I am here to call on your uncle, Lord Abernathy."

"Whatever for?"

"To find out exactly how much my brother is indebted to him." Her clipped tone held none of the hesitation it had before.

"My uncle does not call Kintore Manor

home." Though Abner *was* currently sleeping off his escapades of the day before in Felix's guest chambers, he had no wish for the creature before him to be introduced to Abner's kind.

He moved farther into the room, leaving the door open for propriety's sake. She had come alone from what he could tell. Did the marquess know where she was? Unlikely, just as her younger brother had slipped away to the races.

Felix gestured for Lady Emilia to take a seat, but when she continued to fret and pace, he remained standing, as well.

There was no chance he'd allow his uncle to set foot near Lady Emilia—sober or otherwise—without him present. In fact, he'd been prepared to give his uncle a severe tongue-lashing when he arrived home from depositing Iain. Unfortunately, Abner had had a waiting bottle of scotch hidden in his carriage and had spent his journey from Epsom Downs to London getting thoroughly sloshed. When Felix had returned from Cavendish Square, he'd found Abner slumped in a chair in his study. He'd had no choice but to have his footmen carry the man to the room he'd used when he lived at Kintore Manor with Felix.

He'd given his servants strict instructions to alert him as soon as Abner rose for the day. There was much to discuss, and Felix had no intention of allowing him to slip from the townhouse before they spoke.

"I am not certain my uncle will be willing to assist you." He clutched his hands behind his back to stop himself from taking another step toward her. He knew well enough why he sought to speak with Abner, but Lady Emilia?

Her pinched lips and furrowed brow spoke of her unease.

"If you have other concerns, I can assure you my uncle will not cause your family any further troubles," Felix said; however, it did nothing to alleviate her pained expression. "He will not seek out your brother again. Do speak of this to your father. Give him my word."

"My father cannot know of any of this." She trembled slightly with each word, though she did not strike him as a woman who was frightened of anything, least of all her kin.

It was Felix's turn for concern. "I am certain he cannot miss the injury to your brother's face."

She shrugged, belying her tense stance. "Iain is notoriously clumsy, and he's been known to stumble when he walks."

Silence grew between them as Felix watched her as intently as Lady Emilia spied him. "My brother is indebted to your uncle, and I—"

Felix held up his hand, palm out to stop her. "Anything he owes Abner is absolved."

"What of the bookmaker?" she asked, her brow raising.

"Bookmaker?"

"From The Howling Owl in Epsom." She spoke slowly as if she were worried Felix did not understand her properly. "Iain says a man named Harris keeps their markers, and their loss yesterday has them owing a tidy sum. I am here to learn the specifics."

"I will take care of the note," he replied. It was Felix's way of things: his uncle made messes, and he came up behind to clean them up. When her eyes clouded, Felix suspected he'd said the wrong thing.

Finally, she halted her pacing and crossed her arms. "We will be indebted to no one."

"It is my uncle who is responsible for this situation. Therefore, I will pay the debt. Your family will not be bothered again."

"No, Your Grace." She shook her head, her short locks falling over her ear. Pushing it back into place, she once again glanced over his shoulder. "I thank you for your intended kindness, but that would mean being indebted to you instead of Harris and Lord Abernathy. Neither is preferable nor suitable for my family and me. If you will direct me to Lord Abernathy's townhouse, I will speak with him directly and gather the coins to repay the marker."

The woman was on a mission—a risky one—and if she were anything like him, Lady Emilia would not stop until she found Abner.

"It just so happens he is sleeping above. Please wait while I summon him."

"I thought you said he didn't live here." Her face scrunched as if she were perplexed.

"I had him returned here after I found him and Lord Strathmore at the racetrack. He was in quite a state." Felix stepped out of the salon to find Goodwin, his butler, waiting. "Please, summon my uncle. Tell him to come directly here."

"Of course, Your Grace." Goodwin nodded before hurrying off on silent steps.

When Felix reentered the room, Lady Emilia had stopped at the window that looked out over the back gardens and the mews beyond. She carried herself with the poise of a lady familiar with the demands of society, yet her appearance was not that of the usual debutante, almost as if she eschewed convention.

He cleared his throat, and she glanced over her shoulder at him. For a moment, he couldn't speak, couldn't think, didn't want to break the silent connection between them. When Lady

Emilia's stare landed on him, it was as if she were looking at him but also around him. He'd gotten the same sense the previous day.

He blinked, knowing it was senseless to think this woman he barely knew could see anything beyond what he showed her.

"My uncle will join us directly," he said, working to keep his tone even.

"There is another thing I must ask of you." She turned and moved across the room until she stood directly before him, staring up into his face with an openness most lacked.

"Anything," he mumbled.

"Lord Abernathy—and you, Your Grace—cannot speak of my brother's foolish claims."

For a moment, Felix could not think of what she referred to.

"He cannot foretell the future," she said with a chuckle. But similar to their prior meeting, the sound struck him as feigned—forced. "My father...he has three girls to see wed, and such gossip will jeopardize all of our futures."

"Do you think me the type of gentleman to spread fictitious gossip, my lady?" Felix waited for her response, but when she only held his glare, he continued. "I do not seek to initiate any gossip, let alone any that will come back to tarnish *my* family name."

She took a step back and nodded, apparently satisfied with his agreement.

"I am truly apologetic my uncle drew your relation into such a folly."

"Do not think Iain is wholly innocent in all this, Your Grace," she chided. "He was well aware of what he was doing and the wrongness of it all."

"Yes, however—"

"That much of this debacle is in the past."

"Felix!" Abner's heavy footfalls sounded outside the salon.

Felix would know them anywhere since one boot scraped when Abner walked as if he didn't quite lift his leg enough.

Felix turned to face the door as his uncle entered, his haphazard appearance indicating that he'd been roused from his bed by Goodwin, who, ironically, trailed behind him.

"Why was I awakened at such an ungodly hour?" Abner demanded. "First, you drag me from the races before all my friends. And now, you interrupt my sleep. Did I teach you nothing?"

Felix had half a mind to list the relatively short, useless skills his uncle had taught him: how to lose a fortune, how to drink oneself to ruin, and how to live off the kindness and wealth of another. All *lessons* Felix had no intention of putting into practical use in his own life.

As was the case whenever Felix was in his uncle's presence, his temper began to rise as he never knew what to expect from Abner. With Lady Emilia present, it was imperative that he not allow his uncle to bait him into another argument with no resolution.

"I should have hailed a hackney yesterday and found my way home," Abner blustered before he noticed that he and his nephew were not alone in the room. The way his uncle's eyes—lecherous and brash—traveled over Lady Emilia in her soft green, patterned morning gown had Felix stepping between the pair. "My, my, my…if you had told me I had a female visitor, I would have made myself a bit more presentable."

Felix let his own glare take in his uncle's rumpled attire. His pants, linen shirt, and coat from the previous day still had a healthy layer of filth clinging to them from the racetrack.

"Lord Abernathy." Lady Emilia moved around Felix and gave his uncle a quick curtsy. "I am Lady Emilia Noble. You are acquainted with my brother, Lord Strathmore. I have come to—"

"Strathmore, you say?"

"Uncle," Felix warned.

"What, boy?" Abner threw a frown in his nephew's direction. "She looks nothing like that swindler brother of hers."

"Iain is not a swindler, my lord," Lady Emilia refuted. "I am here to settle his wager and locate the bookmaker who holds the note on the debt from yesterday."

"As I was telling Lady Emilia before you arrived, Uncle, any debt to you is absolved due to the"—Felix cleared his throat, glancing between the pair—"altercation at the racetrack with Lord Strathmore."

Abner's nostrils flared, and his face reddened. "No, no, the debt he owes me is most certainly not absolved. I need that coin for other..."

"For other what?" Felix asked.

"Other investments, my boy." His uncle's irritation waned, and Felix couldn't help but wonder what his uncle wasn't telling him. "I am a lord about town and have my money invested in many ventures. Yes, many ventures, indeed."

More than likely, Abner owed another debt and had planned to use the coin from Lady Emilia's brother to satisfy that note.

Robbing Peter to pay Paul, or so the saying went.

Felix had no other option but to satisfy the debt, lest his uncle seek out the young lord again when Felix wasn't keeping watch on him. "I will handle the money owed by Lord Strathmore.

However, there is still the topic of how much is owed to this Harris fellow at The Howling Owl in Epsom."

Abner rubbed at his stubbly chin and appeared to be making some mental calculations in his head. Felix wagered his uncle was debating how much would pay the debt and still allow him to keep a few pounds for himself.

"Do you not know the amount, my lord?" Lady Emilia asked.

Her high tone made Felix think she longed to ask if the debt was of staggering proportions. Surely, a woman of Lady Emilia's age would not have the backing to satisfy an obligation of any significance.

Abner shook his head as if he felt remorse. "I do not know the exact figure; however, if my nephew would be so kind as to allow me the use of his carriage, I will undertake the task of returning to Epsom Downs to speak with Harris."

"No!" Felix commanded. "I absolutely forbid you from returning to the racetrack."

"That is not necessary." Lady Emilia glanced in Felix's direction at his outburst.

Abner sauntered across the room, enjoying his moment in the spotlight, and sank into the wing-backed chair closest to the hearth. "While you cannot keep me from returning, it is likely not a wise time for me to be seen at the races."

Felix was not a dullard, and he knew well enough that his uncle's words hinted at his expectation that his nephew would return to Epsom Downs, make good on Abner's debts on his behalf, and free up the man to return once there was no danger.

Sadly, due to Lady Emilia's family's involvement, Felix had no other option.

"I will travel to Epsom and speak with Harris," Felix said, hoping Lady Emilia saw it as the kindness he was offering and not him giving in to his uncle's unspoken demand. "I will find the man and settle the debt."

"Very well." Lady Emilia nodded her agreement. "I will come with you. When shall we depart?"

"You cannot come with me," Felix stuttered. "It is not proper."

Her eyes widened, and her hands landed on her narrow hips, her chin lifting several notches as they did. "I did not say I would be coming alone, Your Grace. My maid, Rosemary, will accompany us as my chaperone."

"I hardly believe that improves the traveling situation, my lady." Felix could not allow himself to envision the hours they'd be locked inside his traveling coach for the journey to and from the racetrack...even with her maid present. "Lady Emilia, I cannot allow you to risk—"

"I am afraid I must insist," Lady Emilia said, halting his protest. "This is partly my brother's fault, and I will see everything settled."

Felix knew relatively little about the lady standing before him, although one thing he sensed with certainty was that she would not waver in her decision to accompany him to Epsom.

MOIRE LOWERED TO sit on the blanket she'd spread on the small, grassy patch behind her family's townhouse. The weather was delightful with the sun cresting overhead, and a breeze cool enough to kiss her heated cheeks and blow her loose hair around her shoulders. A small bird, perched somewhere in the strand of trees not far away, chirped robustly. Yes, the avian sang as if it were on a mission, its chosen path selected, and it was determined to see it to completion.

They were much the same, she and the melodic, feathered creature.

Her vision had been clear. And, as her *seanmhair* had always instructed her, she trusted her gift implicitly.

Especially where Em and her future were concerned.

If anyone deserved a future brimming with love, it was Moire's eldest sister.

Was she contrite regarding the role she'd had Iain play in her undertaking? Certainly.

Did she believe her vision would have come to fruition had Iain not been subjected to a blow to the nose? Undoubtedly.

However, the task would have taken much longer to see done, and she was not blessed with the virtue of patience.

She smiled, longing for a looking glass to preview the loveliness of her grin as her lips pulled up into a genuine smirk.

Yes, if Cat were near, she'd be overwhelmed by her sister's sense of self-satisfaction.

Everything was progressing wonderfully, and she foresaw nothing that could stand in her way...errr, nothing that stood in Emilia's and the Duke of Kintore's way to wedded bliss, that is.

"Why are you grinning like a cat with a mouse at the ready?" Cat plopped down onto the blanket, her book clutched under her arm. "You have been acting awfully peculiar of late."

With great disappointment, Moire tamped down her inner glee and relaxed her face enough to appear the bored, leisurely young lady that her sister had expected to find in the family gardens.

"Oh, I was only listening to the song of a quite verbose little bird." In fact, she had no notion what type the songbird was, nor what gender; however, in her mind's eye, it was a little, yellow canary that had escaped from her gilded cage in a fine London home. The melody had already disappeared, the bird having likely moved on. "I think you scared the poor creature away."

Cat narrowed her blue-eyed stare on Moire. "No, that is not what was giving you such joy a moment ago."

Moire giggled, covering her mouth at the spontaneous noise—or at least she attempted to fool her sister into thinking her laughter meant something far different than it actually did.

As they grew older and mastered their individual talents, it was becoming more and more difficult each day to keep anything private. A thought, an emotion, or a simple white lie were discovered as quickly as they occurred.

However, she was determined to keep this as her secret until the deed was done.

The task complete.

The mission a rousing success.

Maybe a short jaunt into the country would be all that was needed for the pair to realize what Moire had seen in her vision nearly a month prior.

"You are up to some sort of mischief, and I will know it now."

Without a doubt, Catriona would not rest until she learned what her sister had planned. Unfortunately, Cat's efforts would prove as futile as Em's interference with her fate.

When Cat leaned close and pinched Moire,

she realized that her grin had returned, wider than before.

"Soon enough, dear sister. You will find out soon enough." She pushed to her feet, turning her face up to catch the midday rays as they blanketed the garden in warmth. "But today is not the day."

"Tomorrow?" Cat prodded.

She looked down at her sister, their face, complexion, and hair a near mirror image despite the two years that separated them. "Mayhap, if all goes as it should."

And Emilia does not fight her fate, she thought.

With that notion lingering in her mind, Moire started back toward the terrace door that would lead to her father's study.

CHAPTER 4

EMILIA CONCENTRATED ON the slight pressure being applied to her open palm, memorizing the details and wracking her mind for an answer as she squeezed her eyes tight. At this point in the game, Moire or Iain would have cracked an eyelid to peek, but Emilia never cheated. Never conceded defeat.

"Draw it one more time," she asked.

As Rosemary, her maid, began the slow outline again, the carriage hit a rut in the road, sending both women off their bench seat. Rosemary even gave a tiny yelp.

Once positioned again, her maid started the game again, her finger making a sharp shape on her mistress's open palm.

"A horse?" Emilia guessed, opening her eyes to see her maid's frown. "I guessed correctly once more."

"As you have the last fifteen times."

Rosemary released Emilia's hand and sat back, focusing her stare not on the far bench, but up toward the left corner of the carriage top. "How much longer do you suppose, my lady?"

Emilia ignored the clear red haze surrounding her maid as she pulled the drape aside to take in the English countryside. Rosemary was competitive; however, drawing, especially on Em's open palm, was not her strong suit. The carriage game had done its job and passed the hours in the Duke of Kintore's carriage as they made their way to Epsom Downs Racetrack. It was a trick her mother had taught her children during their first move from Dalais Forge to Edinburgh to keep them occupied on their journey.

"Your Grace?" Emilia took in the duke where he lounged across from her and Rosemary, his head tilted to the side, and his eyes closed. He did not sleep. She knew that for certain as she'd watched his aura shifting between colors as she and her maid had played their game. When he opened his eyes, she asked, "Do you know when we will arrive?"

When they'd set out from his townhouse in Berkeley Square, he'd been surrounded by a shade of blue that matched Rosemary's at the time. Both her traveling companions were uncomfortable. She was well aware why Rosemary was uncomfortable, but the duke's reasoning was not as apparent.

Slowly, as if he were actually waking from a deep slumber, he moved the drapes aside. "We have nearly arrived, my lady. Shan't be but a few minutes."

Before they'd left, yellow had flared at the edges of his blue aura when he asked after her family. She should have expected his curiosity to be piqued at her ability to slip away from her family's townhouse, her maid in tow, for an afternoon excursion. However, she'd managed it just as easily as Iain had done on his many trips with Lord Abernathy.

Her *seanmhair* had always accused Emilia's father of being overly lax where his children were concerned and, thankfully, that had not changed since her grandmother's passing. He hadn't the gift of their legacy and, therefore, had never truly grasped the danger surrounding their past—or if their talents were ever exposed in the present. Her *seanmhair* had always said that those without the legacy mark could never properly understand the gift and the curse bestowed unto those with them. It was much the same for her father, especially once they moved to London. He'd been enthralled with town life, as had Emilia's mother.

"Thank you," Rosemary replied.

Emilia collected the deck of cards she and Rosemary had occupied some of their time with and returned them to her reticule before smoothing her hands down her skirt. The simple action would remove the wrinkles collected from their hours in the carriage.

Next, she retrieved her glove from the seat next to her and pulled it back on. Rosemary nearly had apoplexy when Emilia had removed it to play their game. Yet, how was she to guess what animal her maid drew on her palm through her glove? It was an impossible feat. Besides, to the normal person, the duke had appeared deeply asleep for most of the journey.

Before long, the duke's carriage pulled to a halt, and the driver set the brake, climbed down, and opened the door.

After the duke had stepped down, he

reached in to take her newly gloved hand and assisted in her descent.

"Thank you, Your Grace."

When the duke moved to have a private word with his driver, she turned back to the open carriage door. Rosemary's frown of disapproval stung. "We will not be long. The duke's driver will be right outside while we are gone."

Emilia had done much to deserve her maid's disapproval. First, agreeing to travel to Epsom in a duke's conveyance. Second, removing her glove in said duke's presence. Lastly, requesting that Rosemary await them in the carriage and not accompany her on their errand.

Her maid would certainly deserve an additional day off that week for her discreet disapproval of Emilia's course of action. And she'd gladly give the woman her due if she promised not to breathe a word of any of it to Emilia's father. Not that her maid, who'd been with her family since Edinburgh, would ever speak of anything her mistress bid her to keep private.

When Rosemary gave Emilia a reluctant nod, she turned back to take in the sight of Epsom Downs Racetrack. Many carriages lined the field around the stables and track with several small buildings taking up space on the fringes. It was all far less...grand than she'd expected. Although there were people of every class milling about, waiting for the race to begin. Men in farmer's garb huddled near a group of finely dressed lords and ladies, most likely from London proper for an afternoon at the races. Even still, a row of boys, no older than Moire, darted past Emilia on their way to the stables beyond. If she'd come for any other reason but to avoid her family's ruin,

Emilia might have moved to the rail with a spot of excitement to partake in the fun.

However, her trip south was not for pleasure.

Unless she counted the hours she'd been afforded an unobserved view of the duke across from her in the carriage. At one point, his leg had straightened, bumping her ankle as his boot slipped under the hem of her gown. She held her breath and prayed that Rosemary did not chastise the lord, but as quickly as he'd extended his leg, he drew it back to his side of the coach.

Her maid hadn't noticed the infraction.

…and Emilia could still feel the press of his leather boot against her stocking-covered ankle. Blessedly, she'd worn her short boots as Moire had suggested. She was the fashionable one of the family, and Emilia rarely discarded her advice. Her sister had also selected her dove grey dress as it would hide the dust from the track well, though the bodice was a bit tight, and the neckline dipped lower than she normally wore.

Emilia realized the duke had been holding his arm out for her.

Her cheeks heated. "Pardon, Your Grace. This is my first time at Epsom Downs, and I must say, it is a bit overwhelming."

Correction—*he* was overwhelming; however, she would keep that information as tightly close to her chest as her bodice was.

She slipped her hand into the crook of his arm and stepped close, ignoring the flare of shimmery pink around him. This was not the place to be distracted by his ever-changing aura.

In the end, she could not help but glance up at him as they started toward a small building closer to the track. His brown eyes sparkled, and he actually grinned. Even the darkened circles under his eyes seemed to disappear. It was a pity he did not smile at her; he kept his eyes trained on their destination.

"I remember my first time at the races," he shared, keeping his stare straight ahead. "Lincoln Racecourse. I was twelve, or mayhap thirteen. Abner brought me. He bought me all the refreshments a growing boy of that age could want…and then he disappeared with his cronies. Left me alone and vanished. It was only when night began to fall, and the temperatures dipped, that I realized he'd forgotten me. I was two days' journey from London, and I was alone without any funds."

Belatedly, Emilia realized his ease was not due to the duke finding a spot of contentment or happiness at the track but something entirely different.

Emilia didn't want to believe the duke's story to be true, but his black, cloudy aura with gold flaring at the edges spoke to the damage that had been done to him as a child. For the first time, she was happy she did not possess Cat's gift for emotions; it was likely she'd be crushed by the pain of the duke's memory.

"That is awful." Her fingers tightened on his arm, unbidden. "What did you do?"

"Well, I found our coach and fell asleep, and I never told my parents about it," he confessed. "Abner stumbled back to the coach at first light, and we returned to London. I told my parents I had a marvelous time. The following year, my mother passed, and not three years later, my father followed her. At that point, Abner was made my guardian, but I had learned my uncle's flaws well, and he never surprised me again."

"You've spent all these years caring for him?"

"Ironic, no?" he asked with a sad chuckle. "He was my guardian, yet I have been his caretaker. I have followed him closely and fixed what he damaged."

Her heart broke a bit to think of the young man the duke had once been, and the responsibilities heaped on him at such an age. Her parents might be distracted with town life, but they had never left their children wanting for anything.

Their pace had slowed to the point where others were walking around them as they hurried to places unknown, kicking up dirt and dust in their wake.

The duke glanced around before calling to a passing man who carried a large satchel. "You, sir."

The man, dressed in loose trousers with his yellowing shirt untucked and no coat to speak of, stopped and greeted them. "Good day, m'lord."

"Can you direct us to The Howling Owl?"

With a toothy grin, the man looked between Emilia and the duke. "What ye be need'n there?"

"We are in search of a man named Harris," Emilia offered.

"Ain't no place for a lady, if'n ye don't mind me say'n," he replied. "But none o' my concern." He nodded to the left. "Pub be that way. Down the road a short walk."

"Thank you, sir." The duke nodded, and they set off once more; this time, a destination in their sights.

It wasn't a far walk, and the farther away they traveled from the track, moving down the rubbished-lined road in Epsom, the less dust and dirt swirled around the hem of her gown.

The Howling Owl was little more than a wooden storefront with no windows and no door. The interior was dim from the lack of light, and only boasted a couple of sconces on the walls. Many of the tables had been taken by those seeking a tankard of ale before the race, though some appeared to have been there since the previous day. The odor of unwashed bodies and stale food made Emilia wish she'd had the foresight to bring a scented kerchief.

The barkeep nodded when they approached but remained silent.

"We are here to see Harris," the duke called over the boisterous noise of the pub. "Is that you?"

The man frowned but tilted his head to indicate a door at the back of the room. "Bets are placed in the back."

Again, Kintore thanked the barkeep, and they started for the back room, weaving through tables and sidling around drunken, staggering men. Emilia stepped over a puddle of ale that had collected on the floorboards to keep her hem from becoming both filthy and wet.

When they arrived at the door, a man lounging against the wall a few feet down said, "Ye need ta knock."

"Ready?" the duke asked.

Emilia could only nod her head in agreement; her throat had closed with hesitation. Perhaps it would have been wise to allow the duke to make the journey alone; however, Moire had assured her she'd seen no danger surrounding the trip to Epsom in her visions. Emilia pushed from her mind that her sister's gift did not show her every aspect of their futures.

It was peculiar that a room in the pub had a door though none was found at the front of the establishment, only a gaping hole to the outside as if the pub never closed for the night.

Swallowing the lump in her throat, Emilia donned her most confident expression as the door swung open to reveal a sparsely furnished room with little more than a table large enough for two, four chairs, a cabinet, and a large ledger with an inkwell and quill. The man inside was not what she'd expected either.

"Harris?" They stepped into the room, and Emilia couldn't help but notice how the duke moved to make certain she was behind him. "Are you the bookmaker for the track?"

The man stood from behind the table, his dress that of a gentleman if not of noble birth. His suit was finely tailored, and his neckcloth had been tied with deft hands. When he stepped around the table and clasped his hands before him, Emilia noted his trimmed nails and ink-stained fingertips. In another life, the man could pass as a London solicitor or a man of business; yet his presence at The Howling Owl left no mistake as to his occupation.

The door latch clicked behind them, and it was then Emilia noticed a large ox of a man behind them, blocking their only exit. Similar to the front of the pub, the small room had no windows, only the door they'd entered through. The floors were swept free of dust, and the boards had recently received a thorough scrubbing.

"I am Mr. Harris." The man eyed them up and down. "Although I am at a disadvantage. You obviously know my name, but I am unaware of yours. I have not seen you at The Howling Owl before, my lord."

"The Duke of Kintore. And this"—he did not move to allow her to step forward—"is Lady Emilia Noble. We have come regarding the debts owed to you by Lord Abernathy and Lord

Strathmore."

Harris's brow rose sharply. "If the pair owes you, as well, my note is to be satisfied first, or they know what will happen."

"They do not owe us anything. You see—"

"And I am not in the business of buying other debts." Harris moved back behind the small table and took his seat. "I am busy, with many waiting to see me. The race begins in two hours' time, and there are wagers to log. If you will excuse me."

The intimidating man behind Emilia made to open the door.

"Please, wait," she said, halting the man before stepping around the duke to face Harris. "I am here because Iain—Lord Strathmore—is my brother. I wish to learn how much he owes you so I can settle his debt."

"I do not accept wagers with women," Harris said, pulling his ledger closer.

"I am not here to place a wager. I am here to *pay* a wager. Certainly, you see the difference and are willing to make a small concession to your rules." What would they do if the man refused to give them the information they sought? The journey would be for naught, and they would return to London in the same position as they'd left it.

"We only seek the totals," the duke said at her side. "That is all."

Harris's glare narrowed on them. "My clients would be very disagreeable to my speaking of their private matters."

"My brother hasn't the funds to pay his debt," Emilia said, her shoulders straightening as she did her best to match the man's menacing glare. Unfortunately, her small stature did not allow her to look down her nose at the man but rather directly at him. "If you do not give me the amount, you will never see the debt paid."

"Harris always gets his money," the man behind her hissed.

Emilia maintained her stare, refusing to look away and break eye contact.

Finally, Harris sighed. Collecting a pair of spectacles from the desk, he slipped them on, licked his thumb, and began turning the pages in the ledger.

"Abernathy...Strathmore...Abernathy...Strathmore..." Harris scanned the page until his finger pointed at a specific entry. "Most unfortunate."

Emilia inched forward, and she could feel the duke's breath on her cheek as he did the same, but the writing in the log was indecipherable from their angle. The room grew overly warm as she waited for Harris to speak again. Mentally, she stopped herself from wracking her brain on how she'd find the funds to settle the debt without her father's help—or the duke's charity.

"It appears Lord Abernathy's good-luck streak has finally come to an end," Harris said with a whistle.

"How much?" the duke demanded.

"One hundred and twenty pounds." Harris glanced up from the ledger. "I do not accept cheques or directions to your lofty solicitors in London. Paper notes only."

"And Lord Strathmore?" Emilia asked. There was little chance she'd ever be able to repay such a large sum, not even with her father's help. Her allowance was mere shillings a month, and even if she, Moire, and Cat collected all their pen money and sold their finer dresses at the market, they would never amass even half that amount.

Her blood hummed in her veins, and her head began to pound as Harris tapped the page.

"Fifty-seven pounds," he answered.

It wasn't as staggering as Lord Abernathy's debt, but still more than she could hope to collect.

"How long until it is due?" she asked.

"Yesterday."

"Yesterday?" she gulped.

"Wagers are to be made good on the same day, just as I pay out winnings," he confirmed. "I don't suppose Abernathy and Strathmore plan to be added to my blacklegs list, do they?"

"What is a black—"

The duke placed his hand on her elbow to silence her. "We will need to see a banker to collect the funds," he replied.

"Gunther runs the Epsom Holdings and Treasury in town." He paused and retrieved his timepiece from his jacket pocket and flipped it open. "However, bank closes in fifteen minutes as he is a patron of the racetrack himself."

"I will need to collect the money from London," Emilia said, praying the bookmaker would show her a bit of leniency. "I can return on the morrow."

"It can all disappear as easily as it appeared," Harris said, slipping his timepiece back into his pocket.

"What do you mean?" the duke voiced her question before she could collect the sense to piece the words together coherently.

The man scanned his ledger once more. "The pair have another bet on the log for two days from now. If they win, their debts will be satisfied with some to spare."

"And if they lose?" she whispered.

Harris shrugged as if it were of little concern

to him. "They will owe a queen's ransom—to me."

The bookmaker's aura had remained consistent through their entire meeting. "He speaks the truth," she mumbled.

"Of course, I speak the truth." Harris slammed the ledger closed and stood, tucking the tome under his arm.

"I wish to cancel the bet," the duke's voice thundered off the bare walls.

"You cannot withdraw another man's bet, Your Grace, duke or not." The bookmaker stepped around the table until he stood before the duke. "I would not be the businessman I am today if I allowed such backhanded dealings." With a sigh, he stepped around them and pivoted. "Besides, Abernathy was quick to speak of Strathmore's skill at selecting horses. I even heard a rumor that Gussy at Epsom Downs was looking to possibly offer the young lord a post with the track. However, their recent turn in luck likely did away with his faith in the boy's talents."

"My brother has no such skill," Emilia countered.

"My uncle, nor the young Lord Strathmore, can settle their markers," the duke said as a grey haze wavered around his person. "Perhaps, with time, I can—"

"No." Harris's hardened glare moved from the duke to Emilia where it lingered for longer than she was comfortable with. "I have heard all this before. I think the pair of you are here to distract me from what is really afoot."

"And what is that?" Emilia gulped. The room closed in around her as she attempted to reconcile what had gone awry with their meeting.

Instead of answering her question, the bookmaker posed a question of his own. "Where are Lord Strathmore and Lord Abernathy?"

"In London." The Duke of Kintore crossed his arms over his chest. "As I said, we have come to learn what is owed so we can make good on their lost wagers."

"I think, Your Grace, I am being swindled by those two blacklegs." In the time it took the man to exhale, his demeanor had shifted from reserved and intelligent to furious and impulsive. His stare flared with an anger Emilia did not think the situation merited. "You will both wait here while I send my associates to collect Lord Abernathy."

Emilia could think of no retort, insightful nor petty, to throw at Harris as he left the room, slamming the door closed behind him. Staring at the wooden panel, Emilia heard a clicking sound before Harris and his goon retreated.

They'd been locked in.

Locked in.

"His associates?" Emilia turned to the duke, her arms suddenly shaking. "What does that mean?"

He dragged his hand down his face before easing onto the chair opposite the one Harris had been using. "He is going to send one of his men to find Abner and Iain."

"And then what?" The hair on her arms stood up. "Neither can pay what they owe."

"Would you rather know the best-case scenario or the worst?"

Her eyes widened.

"If they find Abner, which is likely to happen, they might attempt to threaten him to collect their money." He paused, and Emilia sensed that what he'd just said was the best they could hope for. "If our luck decreases any more, we are likely to be ransomed, which Abner will not have the funds for. Or, we may be killed."

"Your Grace," she stammered, "you are a duke. They cannot think to murder a duke."

He leaned back in his chair, and the space around him glowed an orangish-yellow. He was working through their problem, hoping to find a solution that saw them both home alive. Emilia didn't need Moire to understand that much.

Taking in the room, nothing had changed from her earlier observations. One door. No windows. A table and chairs. That was all. Harris had even taken his ledger with him when he departed.

Emilia turned and slammed her fist against the locked door. The wood panel was thick and sturdy on its hinges, not even rattling when she pounded her fist on it again. Next, she tried the latch, but once again, she was met with failure.

Outside, the din of the growing crowd increased as sounds of laughter and carousing drifted through the thick door.

She primed herself to scream.

"It will be of no use," the duke said at her back. She turned to face him, her dressing down on the tip of her tongue. "I cannot think that this pub and this room, specifically, were selected for any other purpose but the one we currently find ourselves in. The walls are thick, the door is thicker, and the pub patrons will not come to our rescue."

"So, we sit here and wait for Harris to come back?" she demanded, her anger rising. "I came to settle a debt, not be waylaid by a blackguard...and murdered."

Why hadn't Moire seen this was to happen? In fact, why hadn't her sister warned her about the trouble Iain would find himself in?

"Why are you not more upset about this turn of events?" Emilia stomped around Harris' desk, checking for any drawers that could hold something that might assist them in escaping or defending themselves when Harris and his goon returned. However, the desk was little more than a table—no drawers, no hidden compartments. Nothing.

"Harris will not kill us, no matter how satisfying it might be for him. He wants money, and funds do not come from dead dukes." He nodded at the chair she'd pulled away from the table during her search. "Sit."

"We do not have time—"

"We have nothing *but* time," he corrected. "We will not leave this room until Harris is ready to let us out. There is nothing we can do but wait...and hope he makes his return before we are both so ravenous and thirsty that we look to each other for food. I can assure you we are not the first to be locked in this room. Harris's men know their job well enough to secure us here. And unless that door"—he nodded toward the only exit—"opens, we are going nowhere."

Emilia's eyes narrowed at him. "This is not a jest, Your Grace."

"My apologies if I gave the impression this situation is anything but quite serious, my lady." He gestured to the chair again and waited for her to sit. When she did, he continued, "What I meant is that there is little doubt we will be here for some time, and wasting our energy pounding on the door or screaming will get us nowhere but face-to-face with a very irritated bookmaker. Is that what you want, Lady Emilia?"

"Of course, not." Her indignation was difficult to hide.

"Well, we are both aware that Harris, above all else, wants his money—anyway he can get it...from Abner, Iain, our families, or selling us as horse fodder." He chuckled. "Now, I jest. Harris wants his money, and if he can't get it from my uncle, we—more likely *I*—am his only recourse."

"Are you saying he truly won't kill us?" She watched him intently for any signs of deception.

"Kill, no." He shook his head. "Harm...possibly. However, I highly doubt he'd lower himself to injuring a lady."

She noted that he made no proclamations for his own well-being.

Across from her, the duke reclined in his chair, stretched out his legs, and crossed his ankles. If she hadn't known their dire predicament, she'd think he was but a lackadaisical lord wiling away some time before he was called to dinner. All the while, Emilia's palms had begun to dampen, and her mind was swirling with dread.

CHAPTER 5

THE ONLY SHINING light, as there were no windows in the dank, stuffy room, was that Lady Emilia Noble was not prone to fits of hysteria. While she'd taken her moment to try the latch and explore possible escape ideas, even giving the door a sound thumping and readying herself to scream, she'd ultimately calmed quickly and taken his advice.

Over the years, Felix had encountered men such as Harris on several occasions—all pertaining to Abner—and never had he been gravely injured.

Threatened. Harassed. Pummeled.

Yes.

But never maimed.

Across from him, Lady Emilia lifted her head from the desk where he'd suspected she had fallen asleep as they waited for their captors' return and caught his stare. It was difficult to tell with no view of the outside, but Felix suspected that at least three hours had passed. Depending on their mode of transport, a single ride on horseback could have them reaching London in just over an hour if the journey was swift, and no inclement weather was encountered.

"How are you so at ease?" Her blue eyes took in his relaxed posture.

"It is easy enough to find peace when you know there is naught you can do about your situation," he replied.

He did not tell her he'd visually inspected the room before Harris departed, barring them inside. He was well aware that there was no method of escape unless the bookmaker returned and unlocked the door.

The swell of activity in the main pub told him that the race had ended, and the patrons had returned to their watering hole for ale and a sparse meal. Felix's stomach ached at the thought of food, even a stale, crusty piece of bread and a tankard of water would be welcomed.

As if reading his mind, she said, "How long do you think it will be? As you feared, I am starving. Do you think Harris' associate is outside and will bring us a meal?"

"No one has the key but Harris." He'd spoken the truth when he told her that no one would come to their rescue. "He is far too skeptical, even of his own men, to leave a means for us to escape before he has his money."

Felix stood, his legs aching as he paced the small room from wall to door and back again.

"Do you think they will find Iain?" The trepidation in Emilia's voice had Felix halting and turning to face her. "It is just...he is only a young man. He cannot defend himself as we can."

Felix smiled. "As *we* can?"

"I am more than capable of caring for myself in a situation such as this." Her shoulders stiffened, and she brushed a short lock of blond hair behind her ear.

"May I ask you a question, Lady Emilia?"

Her blue eyes narrowed. "Of course."

He took a deep breath, preparing to broach the subject that had seemed to be forbidden from their first meeting. "Earlier, you said that Harris wasn't lying about Abner and Lord Strathmore owing a queen's ransom if they lost, but you did not say you *thought* he wasn't lying. There was a measure of conviction in your tone that I am unfamiliar with."

"Your question?"

What was he attempting to ask? Lady Emilia's reaction to Abner's insistence that Iain could accurately predict the winner had been one of outright denial, to say the least. She'd been quick to call anyone who believed such nonsense a fool. Yet, her exact words had been that *Iain* could not predict the future, not that it was impossible for another.

He shook his head and pivoted once more, pacing away from her. "My question is how do you know that Harris wasn't lying? And how can you be so certain Iain has no gift of foresight?"

Even the words sounded wrong when he verbalized them. Foresight?

It was lore from the past—a witch's curse.

No sane person could actually believe that such a skill existed and that someone they knew possessed it.

"Come now, Lady Emilia," he said, turning to return to his chair. He sank heavily onto the seat and stared at her across the desk. When he leaned closer, she instinctively tilted away. "We are in this situation together. I cannot rectify it if we are not honest with one another."

Felix was not irrational enough to think Iain had any special gifts. Nor deluded enough to believe that anyone but Harris could rectify their current situation. More likely, Lady Emilia's brother might know someone at the track. Perhaps he had been given information about the horses who were to race and used that knowledge to place his wagers.

Emilia watched him closely but said nothing.

"I am fully aware how I've found myself in such a position. My rakehell uncle has a penchant for gaming, drinking, and making poor life decisions. He has never been a particularly wise man who values self-preservation. If it were not for me—and my parents before me—Abner would likely be locked in debtor's prison." He hadn't meant to share further harsh family realities with her. "But how did you get here? What of your brother? Has he always thrown caution to the wind and jeopardized his own safety?"

"Iain has always been different than my sisters and me."

"He has routinely sought out risky endeavors?" Felix prodded.

She shook her head. "No, that is not what I meant at all."

He glanced toward the barred door, hoping averting his stare would give her a moment of privacy to collect her thoughts. The even, unending drone of the pub had faded into the background hours ago, serving to remind Felix how quiet and still the room was.

"Iain has always been on an unspoken journey, desiring a place to fit in when he so clearly is out of place in his own family."

"Because he has all sisters?"

Lady Emilia chuckled. "I wish it were that easy to explain."

"We have time," Felix mused, not wanting to push her to say more than she was comfortable with sharing. There was so much from his past that he'd never spoken about with another—and never would. "And I am told I am a superb listener."

Sitting back in his chair once more, he feigned indifference; yet his chest froze in anticipation.

"My sisters and I, Moire and Catriona, we have a bond my brother is not a part of." She glanced up at him as if she feared his reaction to her confession. "It is not because we do not long for him to share our bond or to join us. However, it was not fate's plan for him."

"I suppose Iain and I have much in common where fate is concerned."

"How so, Your Grace?"

"My given name is Felix," he said.

"It is not proper, Your—"

"I believe we left propriety back in London, or perhaps with your maid and my driver in my waiting coach." He smiled, hoping to alleviate her misgivings. "It is only you and I, Lady Emilia. And I am requesting we do away with formalities, at least until we find safety."

Felix sensed when she conceded because her frown eased slightly. "I forgot about Rosemary. She must be dreadfully worried that we haven't returned."

"My driver will care for her properly until we are freed."

"Mayhap your driver will come for us." The hope in her tone was nearly too much for Felix to bear. "He could be in the pub right now..." She leapt from her chair and hurried toward the door, her fist raised. "If he is looking for us, he will hear our pounding on the door and demand our release."

He allowed her to thump on the door several times before he halted her. "My driver is not looking for us."

It was Felix's one regret.

Lady Emilia swung around to face him. "You cannot know that."

"But I can."

"Why would he not come in search of us?" Her voice cracked on the last word.

"I told him not to." In hindsight, the command sounded foolish and suspect.

"Why would you do that?" Her hands fell to her sides as she gawked at him.

"It is best I handle my uncle's problems alone," Felix said for lack of a better explanation. "You are only present because you insisted on coming."

"I cannot... What if? Oh, I can only imagine the desperation Cat is feeling right now," Lady Emilia stammered as she lowered herself back into her chair. "She must be so frightened for me."

"Your family cannot know our current troubles, my lady," he reassured her. "Just as my driver remains unaware."

"If we are to waste away in here alone, you may call me Em—or Emilia," she said. "Whichever you prefer. And, as I said before, my sisters and I share a special bond. They are alone in London, without me, and they must be scared." She set her hands on the table and clenched them tightly to stop her fingers from trembling. "What if Harris and his men go to my home and take Iain? What if they already have him, and he's admitted he has no money to repay his debts?"

Perhaps Felix had spoken too soon when he determined she was not a lady prone to hysterics. If Harris returned with her in such a state, she could act out of turn and further infuriate the bookmaker.

"Felix, are you certain he will not harm us?" Emilia whispered.

"He wants his money," Felix replied, concentrating on her question and not the sound of his name on her lips. "Above all else, he wants the debts settled. After they are, we will never see him again, I can promise you that."

"You speak the truth, but I cannot understand how you can be so certain," Emilia mumbled.

"I can be certain just as you seem to know I speak the truth." Yet, he could be sure no more than she could know he hadn't lied.

"I suppose that could be so." She bit at her lower lip, but her hands eased.

Felix searched for a way to distract further from her worry, despite her hesitancy to speak on the matter of her family. "Why would Iain make such promises to my uncle?" He'd wondered about that since delivering Iain home the previous day. "It is a peculiar claim to make, especially with such high stakes as horseracing. He must have known if he failed there would be dire consequences."

Emilia stared at Felix closely as if she were assessing him in that way she did when she looked at him yet around him.

Finally, her small, upturned nose scrunched, and she exhaled a large breath as if she'd been holding it in for some time. "I can only guess at

Iain's reasons; however, I can assure you that he holds no special gift. Yet, at the same time, I'm sure he believed he'd chosen the correct horse."

"He was correct many times. How can you be certain he holds no gift?" he asked. "There has been lore of those who hold powers of the occult, who practice the art of magic and will curse those who cross them."

Felix chuckled at the last part, expecting his outlandish words to elicit at least a laugh from Emilia. When she remained stone-still, and her frown returned, he sat up a bit straighter, fearing he'd offended her.

"What if he is a witch. Or, not a witch, but a man bestowed with a rare gift?"

"I, well…" He fell silent, no answer to give.

"Would you tie him to a stake and set fire to him?" she demanded.

"What?" Felix was taken aback by the venom in her words. "You cannot be serious."

"I am deadly serious, Your Grace." She stood, placing her gloved hands palm-side down on the table as she leaned toward him, her once peaceful blue stare now filled with turmoil. "Do you think a curse plagues those with abilities?"

"I have never known someone with any such abilities," he countered. "I cannot say I have ever given the notion any thought. However, I have never, *will* never, seek to injure another."

Emilia leaned several inches farther across the table, holding his bewildered stare.

"I have spent the better part of my life making certain my uncle causes no harm to himself and others," he retorted, his temper rising at the notion that she'd think him capable of such brutal actions. "I would do no differently with Iain—or anyone, for that matter, be they pauper or prince."

After another long moment, she pushed away from the table, seemingly satisfied with his answer. She stalked across the room, swung around with a jerked motion, and paced back toward the door—on the same path he'd taken only a few moments before. It was similar to the way she'd appeared when he walked into the blue salon at his townhouse. She, muttering to herself as if weighing some unknown options in her mind.

"I can be certain Iain does not have the gift of foresight because it is my sisters and I who were gifted the Dalais talents." She lifted her blue stare to his, her inner battle gone as the turmoil receded. "But we are not witches as one normally thinks of those who command sorcery."

His first reflex was to laugh. He'd sought to distract her, and it was Emilia who was distracting him with stories of fancy.

However, something in the set of her shoulders and the lift of her chin stopped him.

"What are you saying?" Felix was uncertain he wanted to know.

Again, Emilia remained silent, seemingly waging war within herself before she halted before him. "We three were gifted with the legacy mark of the Dalais trio: three triangles that make our family symbol when overlapped. With the mark, we were given gifts: premonition, empathy, and I can gauge a person's aura and discern their honesty."

"You jest," he blurted.

Her stare hardened once more. "Do you doubt me?"

"I have never believed in such things," he said. "I cannot doubt nor believe what I have never experienced."

"You wondered how I was convinced that

Harris told the truth. Well, it is my gift."

The topic bordered on fantasy. Yet, something about Emilia told him that she wasn't lying, or at least speaking the truth as she knew it.

"My *seanmhair*"—she paused as if *seeing* his confusion—"my grandmother, she had the gift of all three, a rarity in our family history. My father says she was cursed—the past, the future, emotions, and auras—it was certainly a burden, yet one she accepted with zeal. She taught my sisters and me much before her passing. Unfortunately, my siblings are still young and do not always use their gifts wisely."

An idea popped into Felix's mind, and it was as if he were suddenly catching up on what Emilia had been trying to tell him. "One of your sisters was telling Iain which horse to wager on."

"Yes, Moire, she has the gift of foresight."

"And your other sister?"

"Catriona has an empathic gift with emotions," she confessed.

"How is that different from your gift?"

Emilia let out a light laugh as if the difference should be obvious. "I can see, or rather *read* a person's inner feelings, something they, themselves, are unaware of. Catriona *feels* their emotions as if they are her own, though she does not know why a person feels the way they do. My gift takes little energy or concentration on my part, while Cat's ability is draining physically, mentally, and emotionally."

"Are you reading me now?" His heartbeat sped up until he had to clamp his mouth shut to slow his breathing.

"I am always reading others." She took a step toward him, so close she could reach out and touch him—and she did. She ran her gloved finger down his arm, and he pushed to his feet, almost as if he were at a disadvantage if he remained seated. "The yellow around you says you are curious about my gift, though it swirls with a darker brown at the edges, meaning your common sense is in opposition to your curiosity."

She smiled as she looked down and slowly removed the glove from her hand, pulling each finger until her hand was exposed and she slipped the material free. With aching deliberateness and intention, she raised her hand and set her palm on his cheek.

"And now?" he said on an exhale.

She tilted her chin up until Felix felt her warm breath caress his neck as their eyes held. If it were true, she could see his emotions, but he could read hers just as clearly in the sapphire orbs of her eyes. Whatever traveled between them, making it impossible for him to look away, shone brightly in her stare. There was no doubt that she was as aware of the connection between them as he was, drawing them together.

Felix knew the wisest course would be to look away and put as much distance between them as the small room would allow until Harris came to release them, yet he was helpless to step away from her. His boots were rooted to their spot on the wooden floor. Her touch upon his cheek was everything he'd lacked all these years. The unfamiliar scent of her so close to him was a welcoming blanket he hadn't known he needed even in the warmth of the small room.

Suddenly, he was exposed in a glorious yet terrifying way.

Lady Emilia could read him; however, he was unable to gauge the emotion behind her intense stare.

Far too soon, her hand fell away from his cheek, and she took a measured step back, the distance between them feeling monumental, not the mere few inches it actually was.

Had he done or said something wrong—or worse, *felt* something wrong?

CHAPTER 6

EMILIA DREW IN a deep breath at the same time she took another small step away from the duke—Felix. She knew she needed to put distance between them just as she was sure she could trust him implicitly.

What she did not understand was the shimmering deep pink surrounding him. It had only grown more potent when she placed her hand on his cheek. She'd never seen such a thing. She'd learned long ago that a person's aura was never static; it flowed, ebbed, and altered with the moment; however, she'd never before witnessed the deepening of an aura to such a degree.

She was not daft, her *seanmhair* had taught her enough to know arousal when she saw it, but Emilia had been utterly unprepared for the intensity of it or for the fact that she'd reciprocate, her body responding to his desire.

Then the pink began to fade, overtaken by a blue so pale it made Emilia long to return her hand to his jawline or her fingers to his arm.

There was nothing that could have stopped her, no warning shouted from the highest mountain that would have changed her course. Emilia stepped forward and pressed her body against his.

"Felix," she whispered as the blue faded, returning to the pink that had flared her own desire.

She pushed to her toes at the same time he bent down, their mouths meeting as if two magnets drawn together. For not the first time, Emilia was content that she did not possess Cat's gift for emotions because the magnitude of her own at present was nearly enough to have her legs giving way beneath her. To feel Felix's desires as well would be too great of a burden to bear.

No, not a burden. This feeling that coursed through her was a gift, never a burden.

Her lips moved against his in a steady rhythm, and she focused on the movements, barely noticing when he took hold of her hips, his fingers gently kneading in time with their kiss. It was everything yet nothing like anything she'd longed for—or even dreamed of experiencing.

Emilia pulled away from him with a suddenness she did not understand.

A new color blossomed around him. Green, bright and deep like the grassy knolls surrounding Dalais Forge.

"Emilia?" His murmur came as he opened his eyes, deep pools of dark brown that she could lose herself in. She was already halfway there.

Her *seanmhair's* warning returned in that

moment: *trust your gift, trust your family, but all others should be held at a distance.*

Friend to foe with swiftness.

Lover to adversary.

Yet, she could never imagine Felix as such.

The battle within her started anew.

"You are honest, strong, and caring," she said. "However, those can sometimes be very dangerous things when combined."

His aura quickly shifted to a color of protection—for himself or for her?—and she wondered what her words had meant to him or what he sought to keep from her. There was no doubt he was attracted to her, and she to him. But there was something more, something far stronger beneath his attraction.

The Duke of Kintore more than desired her…he was utterly enamored with her.

It was the green shared by her parents. The hue that had always surrounded her *seanmhair* when she looked upon her four grandchildren.

But Felix barely knew her and had only begun to hear all her entanglements. There was much more to her family and their past than she'd ever be comfortable sharing with another.

Suddenly, the bolt on the door was released, and the latch jangled as the door swung inward.

"Your Grace! I have been searching everywhere for you despite your insistence that I wait by the coach."

Felix stepped away from Emilia as she swung around to see the duke's driver, Jameson, standing in the open doorway. Rosemary stood behind his imposing frame, wringing her hands.

"We should be going," the driver said, glancing over his shoulder into the crowded pub. "The coach is waiting outside."

The duke's hand pressed to the small of

Emilia's back as she clumsily slipped her hand back into her glove before Rosemary noticed.

They made quick work of exiting the pub, keeping to the sides of the room before exiting the establishment altogether, no sign of Harris or his goon. Jameson didn't bother waiting for them to enter the coach before he clamored up to his perch and released the brake.

Felix assisted Rosemary up and then Emilia, his hand squeezing her with reassurance before letting her go and jumping in himself.

The coach took off toward London as Felix pulled the door shut.

As Emilia eased back into the plush squabs of her seat, a laugh escaped her.

"My lady," Rosemary said, breathing heavily from their sprint to the coach. "I was ever so worried. I thought grave harm had come to you, and that I would need return to London to tell the marquess."

Emilia's mind swirled with everything that had transpired in Epsom: her captivity, the danger, the staggering debt...but her thoughts always returned to Felix and their kiss.

She'd never experienced a connection so strong, except that which existed between her, Moire, and Cat.

This mission was no longer about protecting her family, it was now about seeing that Iain was not in danger.

"I have a plan," Emilia said, catching Felix's eyes across the carriage, longing to sit next to him and not her maid. "I cannot risk Harris or Lord Abernathy speaking about my family, and we cannot allow Iain or your uncle to be harmed. You have said that Harris will leave my family alone once the marker is settled, correct?"

"Yes." Felix frowned, and Emilia didn't need

to check his aura to know that he was leery of her plan, even before hearing it. "I have already decided to meet with my solicitor when I arrive in London to have all the debts settled immediately."

"I have a better idea. It will repay all our debts and not have my family beholden to you." As her plan took hold in her thoughts, Emilia settled in for the long journey back to London, safely ensconced in Felix's coach. His eyes were upon her, studying her, but she didn't care overmuch.

Emilia would settle Iain's debts *and* win back her family secret. After that, she would see if anything remained between her and the Duke of Kintore.

EMILIA DIDN'T WAIT for Edwin, their family butler, to open the front door, she just pushed her way in, Rosemary hurrying to keep up with her mistress's strides. Their journey back to London had been uneventful. With her maid next to her, Emilia hadn't been able to speak with Felix about what had transpired between them at The Howling Owl, nor explore her upcoming plan to remedy everything. Her mind had been preoccupied with how she'd pose her idea to Moire to secure her help, though her youngest sister was as much to blame for Iain's predicament as her brother was.

The hours spent locked in Felix's coach had served one purpose: to reignite her anger at Iain for placing them all in such a precarious position. For leading Emilia to break a promise she'd made to her *seanmhair* so many years ago. And for the lack of guilt she felt at the betrayal of her family secret to Felix.

Catriona ran into the foyer as Emilia shrugged from her cloak, but her sister skidded to a halt as her face paled to a ghostly white. *This* was something Emilia did feel remorse over. Her fury and anger coursed through her sister, but Emilia would not let go of her current mood.

"Are Mother and Father home?" Emilia demanded.

"N—n—n—no," Cat stammered as Moire came into the foyer. "They are at Lady Heston's residence for the evening."

A measure of relief flooded Emilia. Her father being away gave them a bit more time to handle the situation without the marquess learning of it. Iain would surely be punished, and they'd all have to pack their belongings and move on, away from their home once again.

Away from Felix.

Emilia pushed the thought from her mind.

She needed to gather her siblings to help satisfy Iain's debts and make sure the bookmaker—and Lord Abernathy—did not speak to anyone of their family's peculiar gifts. Even if neither man knew the true extent and nature of the Dalais legacy, any word of them and what they could do would spread quickly...and those who hunted her family for generations before would inevitably come.

The mere idea was unfathomable to Emilia.

She hadn't any firsthand knowledge of who those *hunters* were, where they came from, or how they might arrive at her family doorstep, but the continued fear of those childhood memories locked in the root cellar at Dalais Forge, her *seanmhair's* warning still fresh in her mind, had terror overtaking Emilia.

However, there was a far greater possibility that Harris and his men would hunt down her brother and Lord Abernathy and harm them. Still, Emilia could not dispel the fear within her surrounding her family's gifts. It had been instilled in her at an early age. No hunter had been seen for over seventy years, not since before her grandmother's birth, but that fact made them no less real and dangerous to Emilia and her sisters.

"How did things transpire with the duke?" Moire inquired, stepping around Cat where she stood frozen, her auburn locks appearing as if she'd been worrying them for hours. Emilia knew the heightened connection between her and her sisters enabled Cat to feel Emilia even at a distance.

Emilia looked at her youngest sibling; her aura was a deep jade. Moire hadn't asked after Iain's debt, the bookmaker, or why the journey had taken so long. She'd asked after the duke. Did Moire know of their time locked away in the room in the pub? Did she know of their kiss?

Had her youngest sibling foreseen what would transpire between Felix and Emilia before they'd even departed London?

Moire would never keep hidden something of such import, would she? If Moire had seen anything in her visions, Emilia was confident she would have come to her with the knowledge. She had to believe in her sister's veracity—or the truth would be too much for Emilia to reconcile.

"Where is Iain?" Emilia demanded. She would not dwell on what Moire had or had not seen in her visions up to that point. What mattered was what Moire would see in her *coming* visions. When neither sister responded, Emilia inquired again. "Where is Iain?"

"He is hiding in his private chambers," Moire replied offhandedly.

"Are we to assume it did not go well at the racetrack?" Catriona tentatively asked. "You are rather upset, Em. My erratic heartbeat speaks to your unrest."

Emilia stared between her two sisters, the gravity of her escapades finally settling around her. "I was locked in a tiny room at the back of a pub with no water, food, or means for escape— with only the duke as company. The bookmaker threatened both my person, the duke, and our families if the markers were not settled immediately." She took a deep breath, her lungs aching in protest. "Therefore, Cat, it did not go well at the racetrack."

"Are you certain it—"

"Thankfully, I have a plan to rectify everything," Emilia continued, cutting off Moire. She did not want to hear the girl's question nor ponder how deeply she was invested in their current situation. The pair of them would need to work together to set everything to rights without their father finding out. And then, only then, would Emilia question Moire about her hand in Iain's predicament. "And everything will be back to normal in a couple of days' time."

Emilia only hoped Harris and his men did not find their family before she saw her plan to fruition.

"Moire, you helped Iain select the winning horses at the track. You will need ply your talents again for an upcoming race." Emilia gave her sister no time to dissuade her. "I have little idea *why* you gave him the incorrect horse, but we cannot risk that mistake again. I will be going back to Epsom in two days' time, and I will need your selection before I depart."

Cat's eyes clouded with confusion at the confidence radiating off Emilia.

"I will accompany you," Moire replied.

Emilia shook her head. "No, I cannot jeopardize your safety. If Harris spots me, he will also see you. I cannot have—"

"I need to be certain of the victor, am I correct?" When Emilia reluctantly nodded, Moire continued, "I will need to be close to the horses. Only then will I be absolutely certain of the outcome."

"You have not needed that intimate closeness before," Emilia refuted.

Moire's shoulders tightened, and her chin lifted. "There is much at risk with this, sister."

Emilia didn't want to give in to Moire's insistence. Never would she willingly place any of her siblings in danger, though it was unfortunate that Iain didn't have the same way of thinking when it came to his sister.

This would be her only opportunity to repay Iain's debts in full. Her plan had to work, or she'd have no other option but to involve their father and risk her future in London.

Their futures in London.

MOIRE DID HER utmost to assume a look of utter concern—contrived as it may be—least Em discover she was being less than truthful. Judging from her sister's erratic and frazzled appearance, her day spent locked in that small room at the pub had been eye-opening and—dare she say it...enjoyable? For both her sister *and* the duke.

Rosemary appeared sufficiently scandalized

by their time at Epsom Downs.

However, Emilia's determination to return to their normal way of life was concerning.

Life returning to normal was not in *Moire's* plan at all. For now, she would allow her eldest sister to believe that her plot was the only one in motion, though she knew the truth of the matter.

She hid her sly grin as she fled down the corridor to the drawing room.

It was past time that Emilia, and the fate Moire and their *seanmhair* had foreseen all those years ago in the cellar at the Forge came to be. If that meant doing her utmost to propel Emilia along her fated path...then so be it.

Good fortune and blessed fate waited for no man—or woman.

In this case, it meant that Moire would need her visions to be a little less reliable, a lot less clear, and undeniably more imperative. The future was never written in stone, and the choices people made could alter how and when things came to pass, but the end had been decided long ago.

Thankfully, knowing her family would never be in jeopardy of being exposed was a boon her sister did not have.

And that was all due to the Duke of Kintore.

Now, it was up to Moire to make certain Emilia took hold of her fate—and the duke.

CHAPTER 7

FELIX READ THE missive that had arrived the previous evening one last time before crumpling the paper in his hand and shoving it back into his jacket pocket and pacing down the long line of stalls once more. The stables were brimming with riders and stable hands running to and fro in preparation for the upcoming race. Dirt and muck already clung to his boots as a result of the steady shower that had fallen the night before.

Glancing over his shoulder, Felix spotted Jameson standing outside the waiting coach.

Lady Emilia was determined to remedy their situation, and Felix was the last person who would step in if his assistance were unwanted; however, he'd collected the funds needed before departing London to settle Iain's debts—as well as Abner's.

No matter the outcome of Emilia's plan and the upcoming race, when they departed Epsom, any debt to Harris would be satisfied, and the bookmaker would have no reason to cause future trouble for Emilia and her family.

A stable hand led a chestnut thoroughbred out of the stall closest to Felix as another hurried over with the appropriate tack: bridle, reins, and saddle. He watched as the pair rubbed the beast down, making sure the stallion's coat was brushed correctly before settling the saddle on his back and tying it in place.

Shielding his eyes from the glare of the sun, Felix took in the gathering crowd as they took their places close to the rail in preparation for the race.

Lady Emilia should have arrived by now. Had she been waylaid either at home or on the road to Epsom? Perhaps Lord Eglinton had discovered his heir's misfortune and forbade Emilia from continuing on with her plan.

Felix's sense of urgency with regards to the situation grew as he surveyed the stable yard for the thousandth time since his arrival.

He should have listened to his better judgement and spoke with Emilia's father that first day he'd returned Iain from the races. If he'd continued on that course, things might well be settled already, and fear of retribution from Harris and his goons would not still hang over their heads.

"Your Grace!" Lady Emilia's distinctive, melodic voice had Felix scanning the stable yard in search of her petite frame and pale, short locks. "We are here, Your Grace."

Emilia, with a young red-haired girl in tow, moved in Felix's direction and bypassed a group of men. There was no mistaking who Emilia's companion was. If her distinctive hair were not enough, her pale skin and startling blue eyes would have given her away instantly.

She was undoubtedly one of Emilia's siblings. But why had she accompanied her sister?

Emilia's note had said nothing of her bringing along anyone but her maid.

Belatedly, Felix realized that he'd been looking forward to another day in Lady Emilia's company. He shouldn't long to spend more time with her, especially without the benefit of a proper chaperone, but he could not help but think of their time at the pub. Finding the time to discuss their kiss would surely be difficult with her maid present, but with her sister at her side...it would be nearly impossible. However, there were far more important matters at hand than those of the heart.

"Good day." Felix bowed to Lady Emilia before turning to the girl beside her. As he'd suspected from afar, her eyes and complexion were a perfect match for Emilia's, though their hair color varied drastically. "I am the Duke of Kintore, my lady."

The girl's lopsided grin told Felix she knew perfectly well who he was—and what had transpired between him and her sister.

"Moire, the duke is who returned Iain home and accompanied me to the pub," Emilia clarified, giving no hint as to the nature of their advanced acquaintance. She glanced around as if making certain no one listened to their discussion before dropping her tone and continuing, "Once you've determined the winning horse, he will place our wager and collect the coin to settle Iain's debt." Next, Emilia turned to him. "Your Grace, this is my youngest sister, Lady Moire Noble."

"A pleasure, my lady." He dipped low over

the girl's hand and smiled when Lady Moire giggled. "Lovely to make your acquaintance, though I was unaware you would be joining us."

"Moire's gift is not always as clear as it could be," Emilia cut in.

"I cannot be completely certain of the winner, though I suspect that if I am close to the animals, my vision will be more reliable." The girl's stare traveled the length of him as she spoke, and Felix could not help but wonder if it were he who was under scrutiny and not the horses filling the stable yard.

"Very well," he conceded. "Shall we begin? I am uncertain how this is done. Do you need to touch the horses, or merely be close?"

Emilia shared a knowing glance with Lady Moire, and the pair communicated something without speaking a word before the young girl looped her arm through her sister's and began to walk the same path he'd paced a few minutes prior.

"I do not need to touch them. Quite regularly, I have visions of people I have never met and places I've never been," Lady Moire shared. "Em has spoken about the gravity of my choice today, and it was I who requested she allow me to come along. I cannot think of the danger Iain is in if I select the wrong horse. Cat and I were terribly frightened thinking of how horrid it must have been for Em to be barred in that room at The Howling Owl. It is very fortunate you were there to protect our sister, Your Grace. I shudder to think what any of us would do without her."

"Moire—" Emilia warned, glancing over her shoulder at Felix where he trailed in the sisters' wake.

"It was my pleasure to be of service, Lady

Moire," he countered, enjoying the falter in Emilia's step and the stiffening of her shoulders. "If we hadn't been trapped, I never would have learned so much about your family."

"I suspected as much." The girl halted, turning to face a black steed tethered to a post. The animal shifted from foot to foot, its head pulling at the rope until his ebony eyes met Lady Moire's intense blue stare. "Hello, fella." She stepped forward and held her gloved hand out for the beast to sniff. "You are a handsome boy, aren't you?"

"This be Zeus." A stable hand appeared around the horse, brush in hand.

"Is he racing today?" Emilia inquired.

"He be." The boy nodded energetically, causing his hat to slip down his forehead to cover his eyes. "Four 'bouts 'round the track and Zeus has won thrice."

"You are very fast, pretty boy." Lady Moire placed her gloved palm against Zeus's nose, and her eyes drifted shut for a brief moment before she frowned, thanked the stable hand, and started down the path once more, leaving Felix and her sister behind.

Felix held out his arm, and Emilia set her fingers in the crook of his elbow.

As they started after Lady Moire, Felix leaned close to Emilia's ear. "Is this how it works?"

She pursed her lips before shaking her head. "Not usually, although many of her visions come to her in private."

"And you think she will settle on the correct horse?" Felix would be lying if he did not admit that he had misgivings about what Emilia had shared about her family. Special gifts passed down through generations was something he'd never heard of before, and truth be told, something he had a difficult time believing. However, Abner had dragged Emilia's brother into their precarious situation, and he owed the woman the opportunity to remedy it in a manner she saw fit.

They paused several paces behind Lady Moire as she turned to stare into a stall. "She understands the gravity of our situation and will do her utmost to help. It is all I can ask of her."

A groom appeared at the stall door and exchanged a few words with the girl before laughing and disappearing from sight.

Felix looked around the stable yard, reassured to note that they were not the only spectators leisurely walking about, glancing into stalls and speaking with grooms.

As Moire moved away from them, Felix asked, "What did you tell your family of our time at The Howling Owl?" It might very well be his only chance to broach the topic with her.

A serene smile graced Emilia's lips as they begun once more to trail Lady Moire as she progressed down the length of stalls. "The truth."

"The truth?" he asked, his shock evident in his tone.

"Not the entire truth, Your Grace, but enough," Emilia replied. If he did not know better, Felix would think her answer was meant to be coy.

"Your sister knows you spoke of your family's past with me?" His breath held as he awaited her answer. It had appeared as much; however, to avoid any awkward moments, he wanted to know exactly what Emilia had told her sister. "I do not mean to pry, my lady."

"As I said, I was forthcoming without

sharing details of our intimate moment."

Felix was uncertain how he felt about her confession. Did their kiss mean more—or *less*—than the secret held between the pair of them?

"Em! Moire!" The call sounded behind them, and Emilia's fingers dug into the fabric covering his arm as they turned in unison to see Lord Strathmore and another young woman rushing toward them. The pair arrived in front of them, each out of breath. "We have been searching all over for you."

"What are you doing here?" Emilia demanded, taking a step away from Felix as her hands landed on her hips. "Iain, you should not be here. If Harris or his men spot you, I cannot imagine it will go well for either of us. And Catriona...Father will have apoplexy if he returns home to discover all three of us missing."

Felix was stunned at how much the young woman before him looked like Lady Moire—and to a certain extent, Lord Strathmore. Felix had the urge to turn and locate Moire to make sure the woman wasn't playing a jest on him.

"Do not fret, Em," Iain replied. His offhanded manner had Felix's concern growing. The young man was in no way worried about his own well-being. "We left a note for Father."

"And where did you say you'd gone?"

"To Ascot, of course."

Emilia's face reddened, and Felix realized that the pair was teasing her, although she didn't seem to see that.

The two siblings shared a smile before they both laughed.

"I think it best you return to London. Immediately," Emilia demanded.

"I can help Moire," Lady Catriona said with a stomp of her foot.

"It is not fair that we were left at home while you and Moire have all the adventures," Iain continued.

"You have had all the adventures this family can handle." Emilia challenged her brother, daring him to disagree. "And, Catriona, you are too young to be here."

The young woman's chin lifted, once more reminding Felix of Lady Emilia. "I am nearly two years older than Moire."

"And yet, only sixteen," Emilia sighed.

Felix had always been burdened with the responsibility of taking care of his uncle so he'd never truly longed for a sibling, yet his brief time around Emilia and her family had him wondering what it would have been like to grow up with more than just himself and Abner. Would he have banded together with a sister—or a brother—to care for Lord Abernathy?

"Besides,"—the girl matched Emilia's stance with uncanny ease—"my talent is as useful as Moire's foresight."

"I have found him," Lady Moire exclaimed, pulling at Emilia's arm and guiding her toward a pristine white horse standing several stalls down at the end of the stables. "Oh, Cat! Come along and tell me your thoughts."

The group moved in unison to stand before the impressive horse. Though Felix lacked any special gifts to speak of, one did not need them to see that the beast they all beheld was taut with power, agility, and speed.

"He is a confident one," Lady Catriona volunteered, stepping forward to stare into the horse's pale grey eyes. "This is his first race, is it not?"

"Yes'm, m'lady," a boy no older than ten summers offered as he untied the horse's reins.

"Sorrel only met his second year. Pardon, but I must be bring'n him ta ready for the race."

"So be it," Lady Emilia called, turning to face Felix as the stable boy led Sorrel toward the track. "A word, Your Grace." She glanced between her siblings, her stare finally landing on the youngest. "Moire, keep watch on Iain and Cat. Do not let them stray even a foot. I needs must speak with the duke."

Lady Catriona's and Lord Strathmore's grunt of disagreement followed them as he and Emilia stepped away from the group.

"Are you confident in their choice?" he asked.

Her lips pressed into a frown, and her brow furrowed as she contemplated his question. "They have never given me reason to doubt them."

"Are you certain you do not wish me to repay Harris and we can be off, this ploy forgotten, and Iain's debt settled?" It had always been Felix's responsibility to care for his rakehell uncle, so he understood Emilia's need to solve Iain's troubles without creating another perceived obligation. "I shall not require the note ever be repaid."

"No. With the wager, I can settle with both Harris and your uncle, and demand that he never breathe a word about Iain's claims of premonition." She was resolute in her decision, and Felix would not press her further on the matter.

"Very well," he conceded. "I will see the wager placed and meet you near the north side of the track. There is a spectator area with seats for you and your siblings away from the rail."

"Thank you again, Felix." She reached forward and squeezed his hand quickly before dropping it, lest her siblings notice.

He held her blue stare for several seconds. "I am at your disposal, Emilia, anything you desire...you need only ask."

Once again, she looked at him and around him at the same time.

He wondered what his aura told her as her hard stare softened, and her gloved palm raised to rest against his cheek.

"Without you, my family would be in harm's way." Her hand slowly moved down his cheek to his neck before falling away. "Though we shall not owe you financially, I will be forever in your debt for maintaining my family's privacy."

The touch of her hand, even covered in fabric, was a warmth that journeyed straight to his chest, making the void within more apparent than it had been in years. He'd lived all his adult life alone with no close relation except Abner, and never a friend to confide in. But with Emilia, he could speak freely because she'd seen his uncle at his worst yet did not think poorly of him.

As he'd made his way in society, Felix had seen many friends come and go, their attachments to him not borne of something true and abiding but due to what they'd gain by their association with the Duke of Kintore.

A horn sounded.

The connection between them severed.

Lady Emilia Noble hadn't asked him for money, nor did she appear the type hoping to connect her family's name with his. Though she knew much about him, she'd shared just as much—if not more—about her own family.

"The race will begin soon," he said. "Collect your siblings and await me by the north gate. I will place your wager on Sorrel and return as soon as possible."

If he stalled another second, he'd never leave her side.

Instead, he called over her shoulder to her brother, who hurried over.

"Lord Strathmore. Please remain close to your sisters until I return." When the young lord nodded, Felix pivoted and stalked toward The Howling Owl. Harris would likely be angered by his appearance, yet he could not fathom the bookmaker turning down a wager large enough to line the man's billfold for months to come.

CHAPTER 8

EMILIA, WITH CATRIONA on one side and Moire and Iain on the other, sat on the hard, wooden plank bench situated a suitable distance from the racetrack. Dirt and dust still swirled about her, making it difficult to draw a deep breath as men of every station gathered at the railing to watch the coming race. The sun was high overhead, with only enough breeze to move the top layers of dust up into the air.

Several other women had joined them on the four rows of risers to partake in the excitement yet keep a modicum of detachment between them and the stampeding beasts. To pass the time until Felix returned from The Howling Owl, Emilia scanned the gathering spectators. One lady, her fine dress and jaunty hat signifying that she was of grand import, preferred to stand next to the rows of seats. Her aura shone a lemon green—a cheat and a liar. Emilia wondered if she had placed a wager based on ill-gotten information or perhaps she'd accompanied a lover to Epsom Downs and not her husband.

Another woman had chosen to sit but clutched her reticule to her chest in utter terror. Emilia had no need to read the young lady's aura. Did she have her pin money tucked in her handbag? Was she frightened of the horses?

Iain leaned forward, catching her eye with a scowl. "We shall never see anything from here."

"We are not here to watch the race, Iain." Emilia marveled at her brother's blasé attitude. "We came to win back the money you lost, repay Harris, and settle your debt with Lord Abernathy. After that, we will return home, this entire debacle behind us."

"Do not upset Em," Cat scolded Iain, though her stare never left the racetrack.

Catriona attending such a large event would likely cause her to sleep for days. The emotional toll her empathic gift hefted upon her was sometimes too great for the young girl. Emilia feared that London, with its many balls, routs, and social entertainments, would be too much for Cat to partake in on a regular basis once she was old enough to participate in such activities. Though her dedication to their family could never be called into question.

Iain only huffed and crossed his arms. Unfortunately, it was the way of things for their brother. As the only Noble child without the family legacy, he was often divided and left wanting, searching for his own path in life while burdened with three sisters: one who foresaw his every move, another who felt his emotions, and Emilia, who knew when he lied.

Many times, Emilia feared he would leave them when he reached his majority to go off on some lark of folly that they could not prevent, and with consequences they could not remedy.

No doubt she—with Cat and Moire to help— would spend much time saving Iain from himself, in a similar fashion to Felix's care for his uncle.

"If Harris—or one of his goons—spots you, they may very well drag you back to The Howling Owl. They are dangerous, no matter what your misguided beliefs are, and I will not have any of it," Emilia whispered loudly enough for Iain to hear but quiet enough not to be overheard by anyone around them.

She craned her neck to see around the men milling about near the railing. Horses were being led to the gates, and Emilia spotted Sorrel, his bright, white coat reflecting the noonday sun. A breeze swept across the open track, causing the horse's mane to blow to and fro.

The race would begin shortly.

Concern pricked at her resolve as she turned to search for Felix. She hadn't any clue how long it took to place a wager on the race; however, it had occurred to her that Harris might be angry that they'd evaded him two days prior. The bookmaker's goons could be holding Felix now, locked in the room at the back of the pub. However, Felix had once again reassured her that Harris's dealings revolved around money and wagers, and that he would never turn down the chance at such a steep bet, especially when the duke placed the wager in full before him.

Moire reached over and gently squeezed her hand. "The duke will return before the race begins."

It was as if Moire had taken over Cat's gift as she reassured Emilia that Felix was unharmed. In that moment, Emilia realized that no matter how often she took the lead with her siblings, no matter how many times she assumed the burden for the lot of them, without Moire and Cat—and even Iain—they would not be complete. She rubbed at her hip through her underpinnings, her birthmark radiating a heat she'd never noticed before. As she did, Moire shifted on the plank and lifted the hem of her gown slightly to stare down at her stocking-covered ankle, her mark hidden beneath. To her right, Cat cupped her left elbow, gently massaging the area through her muslin sleeve.

Even Iain had placed his hand over his heart, his finger splayed wide. Perhaps their *seanmhair* hadn't been completely correct in her assumption that Iain lacked the connection guaranteed by their legacy marks.

Past Iain, a group of men moved toward the railing, their loud laughter and carousing catching Emilia's notice. The men jostled and stumbled as if they'd come from one of the nearby taverns, their tankards of ale running dry.

Both Cat and Moire leaned into her side. Emilia should have seen the young girls back to their waiting coach as soon as they selected Sorrel as their victor. Epsom Downs wasn't safe, not for Iain or her sisters. She'd witnessed firsthand how unpredictable time in an unfamiliar place could be.

"Strathmore!" An elder man detached from the group, eyeing Iain. "What are you doing showing your face at the track?"

"Emilia?" Cat clung to her arm.

"Lord Abernathy." Emilia attempted to distract Felix's uncle—the same man who'd pummeled Iain in the face. Even now, several days later, her brother's nose still held a greenish tint from the waning bruise. "Lady Emilia," she introduced herself again, uncertain whether Abernathy would remember their meeting. "Lovely to see you again, my lord. I hadn't expected to see you in Epsom."

It was her way of questioning the man about his attendance. He owed far more to the bookmaker than Iain, and it wasn't safe for either of them to be about until their notes were settled. She'd heard with her own ears when Felix had forbidden his uncle from troubling her family and attending the races.

And, yet, here Lord Abernathy was, doing both.

"Well, my nephew, honorable lord that he is, cannot deny me my freedom." Abernathy sobered, his stance becoming a bit more solid as he glanced between Emilia and her siblings. "Oh, I hadn't imagined Lord Strathmore would need the help of women at the races."

Abernathy chuckled, and the men around him joined in.

"Is this the bloke who owed you a small fortune, Abernathy?" A man pushed up close to Felix's uncle, and Emilia spied the haphazard cut of his coat.

Owed? Past tense.

Iain *still* owed Abernathy, at least until the current race finished...unless Felix had gone behind her back and settled the note. Emilia could not believe the duke would do such a thing. If anyone understood her need to handle her family troubles without assistance it was Felix.

"Go on with you, my lord," Iain called over the men's laughter. "Let us watch the race in peace."

"Your time is coming, boy," another man taunted, his eyes hidden under the brim of his hat.

"Uncle Abner." Felix appeared between the group of men, clapping his uncle on the shoulder and steering him away from Emilia and her siblings. "What are you doing here?"

Though Felix attempted to keep his tone light, Emilia heard the distinct warning in his words.

"I am enjoying the race, same as you I'd imagine."

The duke leaned close and whispered something in his uncle's ear. The older man stiffened as Felix continued, too low for Emilia— or anyone—to hear.

Finally, Felix stepped away from his uncle, taking in the group who'd arrived with him. "It was a pleasure, Uncle. I think it best you and your cronies move on."

"We have a perfect view at the railing," Abner's associate called. "Hurry, my lord, the race is about to begin."

Felix held Abner's stare for a moment longer before the older man broke away and joined his comrades just as the horn sounded.

Emilia hadn't expected to see Lord Abernathy; however, the sense of unease she'd felt in the man's presence before no longer held her captive. Perhaps it was the aura of protection and courage that surrounded Felix, diminishing the power of Abner's dark green energy. His uncle harbored deep roots of resentment against Felix. She'd need to warn the duke before they parted ways.

The echoing drone of the horses' hooves drew her notice as Felix came to stand close to where she sat. She could feel his presence, though he'd moved out of her line of sight, blocked by Catriona.

Once again, she was surprised by the stark, uncontrollable reactions flowing through the spectators as every eye was trained on the running horses. Even Moire and Cat had been caught up in the excitement of the moment, both leaning forward.

As Sorrel passed by the cheering crowd, Emilia sighed. Only a few more moments, and their horse would win, their winnings would be collected, and Iain's debts would be settled—once and for all. Their family secret would remain hidden with her sole confidant, Felix, a lord of his word, being the only one in the know.

She glanced over to the dark-haired duke who'd arrived at her doorstep only a few nights before. Never in her wildest dreams had she believed she could trust another so implicitly with her family's future. Yet, her *seanmhair*, despite her caution to be wary of outsiders, had pushed her to trust her gift, and nothing in Felix's aura had ever led her to doubt him or his word.

Emilia trusted her *seanmhair's* teachings.

She trusted her gift.

And because of those two things, she had an immeasurable amount of faith in the Duke of Kintore.

As if sensing her stare, Felix glanced in her direction, his smile reassuring her that all would go well.

Though he didn't have Moire's gift of foresight nor Cat's empathic ability, Emilia believed him.

Felix could have gone against her wishes, traveled to Epsom Downs on his own and settled her family's debt to Harris, yet he hadn't. He'd allowed her to accompany him, despite the danger, and stood at her side when she faced

Harris. Even more, he hadn't questioned her plan to wager one final time, nor her certainty in Moire's selection of Sorrel as the winner.

Her chest tightened. Felix didn't turn away to watch the race, and neither did she.

The thundering of the horses' hooves faded until Emilia could hear nothing but the pounding of her heart.

The rush in her veins drowned out the cheers and jeers of the crowd.

The warmth of the sun overhead was replaced by the heat of Felix's stare.

Shockingly, Emilia longed for the privacy they'd shared in the back room at The Howling Owl. If she had those brief hours back, she would have taken the opportunity to run her fingers through his shimmering brown hair or smooth the dark splotches under his eyes. Next, she'd run her hands down his neck and over his broad shoulders to his arms. Would they hold the strength of mind he'd exhibited thus far?

"Em! Em!" Cat and Moire squealed at the same time, pulling at her arms.

Emilia turned at the same moment Sorrel crossed the finish line.

Unable to stop herself, she leapt to her feet and clapped along with the crowd around her, allowing relief to banish the last remnants of the jeopardy they'd faced as she was swept along with the cheering spectators. It was over. They could repay Harris and Abernathy, and she'd demand Iain never place them in such danger again.

Though her father knew nothing, Emilia would be happy to return to London without looming peril hanging over all their heads. They would remain in town, and one day, Moire and Cat would make their way in society. That alone would hold its pitfalls, but her sisters were wise and cautious, and protecting those who wanted her protection would be far simpler than safeguarding Iain, who wagered his safety without regard.

When Cat slid to the ground next to the benches, Emilia followed with Moire and Iain behind her. She could hardly believe it was over—all of it. In a few short moments, she and her siblings would need fear no one...not Harris nor Lord Abernathy.

"That was exhilarating," Moire whispered.

"I told you the races are a sight," Iain responded with a toothy grin.

"Mayhap we can—"

"Catriona," Emilia cut in. "This is our last time at Epsom Downs."

Emilia sensed Felix's presence at her side before his open palm settled on her lower back, a reassuring and comforting gesture she hadn't realized she needed.

The crowd around them began to disperse gradually. Some leaving the race grounds, while others wandered toward the taverns and pubs to collect their winnings or find a repast before journeying back to London proper. Emilia's stomach was still twisted tightly despite Sorrel's win, and she could not think of eating a single bite, at least not until Harris was satisfied, and they were safely back home.

"Shall we attend business at The Howling Owl?" Felix said into her ear, sending a wave of awareness through Emilia.

She could only nod, not trusting herself to speak as happiness and joy mingled with longing and remorse. After they'd satisfied her family's debt, there would be nothing connecting Emilia to Felix. They would go their separate ways:

Emilia back to her sheltered life at her family's townhouse, and the duke back to…

Their acquaintance was so new, Emilia did not know what Felix would return to. Did he partake in societal functions? Was he active in parliament? Did he spend his holidays at his country seat or perhaps in Bath? Did he hunt while in the country, or prefer solitary activities such as reading or the arts?

Emilia knew little about Felix beyond what she'd witnessed since he'd returned Iain to their townhome with a bruised face. Yet, at the same time, she truly believed she knew the man behind the dark facade. She may have no notion as to his likes and dislikes, but the man beneath it all had never been hidden from her.

His compassion, his confidence, his honesty.

They were all things he could never disguise from her.

"Lady Catriona, Lady Moire, Lord Strathmore," Felix called, catching her siblings' attention. "If you will accompany me to The Howling Owl, I shall handle things quickly and see you all on your way back to town."

Felix held out his arm, and Emilia set her gloved hand on the spot near his elbow that was becoming so familiar to her.

They turned toward the pub but had only made it a few steps before Lord Abernathy stepped into their path, his cronies not far behind. The earl's lip lifted in a sneer.

"Uncle." Felix's entire body tensed, the muscles in his arm tightening.

But Lord Abernathy stared past Felix and Emilia to her siblings trailing in their wake.

"You, boy. You did this," Abernathy spit before taking a menacing step closer to Emilia and Felix.

In reaction, the duke stepped forward, putting himself between his uncle and Emilia and her siblings. Felix and the earl were of a similar height, and their hair was of the same shade of dark brown; however, Felix's shoulders were broad, his legs corded with strength, while Abernathy's body lacked substance, having wasted away due to excessive drink. Even now, he wavered on his feet and made no move to push past his nephew to have at Emilia's brother.

The foul odor of molding wood mixed with a citrus undertone spoke to the caliber of drink Lord Abernathy favored. It had been the same aroma permeating The Howling Owl.

"Uncle, I think it best you depart." Felix glanced past Abernathy, and Emilia followed his line of sight. Sure enough, Jameson was beating a path straight for them. "I can join you this evening for a meal, or perhaps—"

Abernathy's stare refocused on Felix, his glare hardening. "You will not order me about, and all while taking Strathmore's side."

"I have taken no one's side on anything," Felix reassured, moving closer to his uncle.

"Oh, I can see by their smiles that Lord Strathmore has given you a winning horse." Abernathy pivoted toward the group of men who'd arrived with him earlier. He had to speak loudly for them to hear. "I told you, gents, the boy has a gift—"

"Enough, Uncle." The steely edge of Felix's tone had Emilia vowing to never cross the duke. "Jameson will see you home. Now."

"Oh, I do not think so," Abernathy countered in a hiss. "Strathmore owes me, and I will have my money, or I shall tell my friends about Lord Strathmore's siblings' talents."

Moire and Cat gasped behind Emilia, and

she longed to turn and reassure them that nothing of the sort would happen.

If the earl confided in his associates, there would be little that could be done to halt the gossip. Even if there were never any proof of Abernathy's claims, that would not stop the *ton* from viewing her family with suspicion. Her *seanmhair* had warned her how unforgiving society could be, how long their memory lasted when it pertained to scandal.

"Lord Abernathy, please..." Emilia despised pleading with the earl. "Iain has won the funds to repay you. Please, if you will allow us to see Harris at The Howling Owl, I can collect your money, and we will be on our way."

The older man shook his head, weaving on his unsteady feet. "Oh, no. Lord Strathmore owes me far more than a mere wager, my lady. And I aim to collect."

"If you continue in this vein, I will never come to your rescue again," Felix warned.

"If Strathmore follows through on our deal, I will not need your money."

"I lied, my lord." Iain stepped to Emilia's side. "I can no more predict the winner of a race as I can the turn of the weather."

"I have learned as much," Abernathy sneered. "However, these three with you have the power, and if they want to keep their secrets from society, they will help me."

Iain turned to Emilia, remorse and regret lacing his expression.

She wanted to tell him that she knew he was sorry, that he hadn't anticipated Abernathy's cruelty, and that she'd find a way to keep their past where it belonged—hidden from everyone outside their family.

Yet, Emilia was uncertain, even with Felix's

help, how to accomplish keeping her family's legacy a secret and securing a safe future for them all.

MOIRE DID HER best to keep her expression one of concern and terror as Lord Abernathy's threat sank in. It was a turn she hadn't foreseen, yet one that did not worry her in the least. The duke had proven himself an admirable ally for their cause, and she had little doubt that the lord would keep her and her siblings from harm.

Perhaps the situation would not progress any further.

A spark of doubt burrowed deep within her.

She was well aware of the undertaking, as well as the risks, she'd come to face with her plan. However, if the Duke of Kintore did not step up and be the man who'd plagued her visions since she was a babe, she could do no more for him.

Fate was an ironic thing.

She was given the gift to see it, experience it, and come to trust it; however, sometimes, it remained elusive.

Or perhaps it was she who was impatient watching and waiting as fate took its time.

Seanmhair had warned her against pushing fate. She hadn't listened.

Emilia was fated to be a duchess. And not just any duchess. The Duke of Kintore's duchess.

With the powerful lord forever allied with her family, their secret would remain exactly that...a secret.

But it was more than an ally Emilia needed. It was love.

An unconditional love that existed between all branches of the Noble family but was rarely trusted from an outsider.

Catriona stepped to Moire's side, tilting her head as if she allowed her youngest sister's feelings to course through her before she spoke. "Em is terrified, yet you are not."

It was a statement.

She was not terrified nor concerned at all.

The doubt she'd felt a few moments before had dissipated as quickly as it had come.

She trusted her gift, which meant she put her faith in her visions for the future.

"I have witnessed what transpires, and I have faith that fate will see this moment to a satisfactory conclusion," she replied.

"I wish I had your assuredness, dear sister."

She grinned, turning her stare to meet Cat's nervous one. "Allow my emotions to give you a measure of confidence."

With that, she reached out and took her sister's hand, hoping her pledge was felt...and believed.

CHAPTER 9

FELIX TEMPERED HIS fury at Abner. It would not see their situation to a conclusion, and would likely terrify Emilia and her sisters. The urge to take hold of his uncle's arm and drag him from the racetrack was strong, and Felix doubted any of the men standing nearby would stop him, but he sensed Emilia's need to keep the attention away from their party.

Why had he coddled his uncle for so many years?

It was Felix's fault that his uncle was emboldened enough to make such outlandish remarks in public.

The years he'd spent covering up his uncle's misdeeds, of repaying the lost wagers, and convincing swindled men not to take out their anger on Abner had done the earl no service at all. His uncle was the man he was, and no amount of care and protection provided by Felix would change him.

Abner pivoted to face his cronies again, and Felix feared what his uncle would say next. He knew about Emilia's family's gifts—or at least he *thought* he did—and the headache he would cause her family would be far-reaching if Felix didn't put a stop to it now.

Fortunately, it was Harris who had Abner falling silent as the bookmaker stalked toward them across the race yard. His uncle's cronies quickly dispersed, leaving Felix, Emilia, her siblings, and Abner to face the man.

The racetrack was all but deserted with only a handful of coaches waiting not far away as the sun had started its descent toward the horizon. Spectators departed as quickly as they arrived in Epsom Downs, few remaining in the area in favor of finding swift passage back to town.

Abner stumbled back a few steps until his back pressed against Felix. "Harris," his uncle stuttered. "I was coming to see you…to settle my wager from the other day and—"

"And repay the debt placed today."

"Yes, yes." Abner's chin bobbed up and down. "Have you met my nephew, the Duke of Kintore?"

Harris raised his brow and nodded to Felix. "Yes, on two occasions, actually. However, I fail to see how that has aught to do with satisfying your markers."

Felix allowed himself to smile for the first time that day. Lady Emilia may very well have her plan for solving her family's troubles, but Felix knew whenever his uncle was involved, things never went as planned. It had been necessary for Felix to make his own arrangements, not against Emilia but in line with her plot.

"Kintore, my boy"—Abner looked between Harris and his nephew, a wide grin transforming his fleshy face—"handle the bookmaker and let us be off back to town."

When Felix made no move to *handle the bookmaker*, Abner's smile disappeared.

"Come now, Felix, my boy," Abner prodded. "Settle the debt and let us return to London. I believe you wished to share a meal this evening."

Next, his uncle scanned the few men and women left at the track, most likely attempting to find his friends who'd deserted him. His eyes widened as he once again met Felix's hardened stare.

"I can offer no assistance this time, Uncle."

Abner's eyes narrowed, and Felix sensed the shift within his kin. It was the same every time he refused to bail the earl out of trouble or repair whatever damage he'd done.

"You ungrateful, sniveling addle-pate," Abner hissed, spittle flying from his mouth with each insult. "You mean to take this roaring mad wench's side over your own flesh and blood?"

It was the same as it often was. Abner would find himself drunk and in danger, and he'd entreat Felix to aid him, and before the coin so much as changed hands, his uncle was spewing vile insults. That was something Felix would live his life handling; however, Emilia did not deserve such hurtful words.

Abner's shoulders sagged. Next would come a showing of remorse, with a healthy measure of guilt levied at Felix.

"I gave up everything...*everything*...to raise you after your father died." Abner was predictable if nothing else. "My estate lay in ruin after I left home to live with you at Kintore Manor. My crops, my tenants, my land...all of it went fallow. But I knew my duty lay with you and your upbringing. I never complained. I never said a word. And this is how you repay me? By turning your back on me when I need you most?"

Felix knew—had known for years—that Abner's troubles were not caused by him but by his uncle's insatiable need for a life outside of his means. The gaming, the drinking, and the irresponsible decisions hadn't begun when Abner had come to care for Felix. He was aware of this fact, but it had never stopped Felix from fixing the trouble that followed Abner. His uncle was his only kin, his last remaining family member, and Felix had always feared that if he didn't take care of the older man, he would be gone from his life—either by choice or due to unfortunate circumstances.

Leaving Felix utterly alone.

Surprisingly, Felix had no urge to assist his uncle from his current dilemma, however. He owed Harris—and likely his *friends*—and Felix would not come to his rescue this time, even if it meant that his uncle never spoke to him again.

The oppressing guilt that usually came every time his uncle began one of his tirades was absent.

Instead, Felix was filled with the need to protect Emilia and her siblings from discovery. Through them, Felix had witnessed firsthand how a family should act: love without expectation, care without ulterior motive, and faith without any doubt.

One should never have cause to demand love. It should be given freely and generously.

"You care about this wanton more than your own blood." Abner held Felix's stare, suddenly completely sober despite his earlier intoxication.

"You mean to betray me for this group of deranged conjurers?"

Felix hadn't taken a sip of liquor in years, yet his uncle's question had his mind clearing as if he'd suddenly awoken from a night spent imbibing all the Scotch in England. He'd never thought of abandoning his only relation for another—least of all, a woman.

However, Emilia was more than any woman he'd ever met.

She was courageous in her fight to secure her family's safety.

He'd never been brave enough to save his uncle from himself.

Yet, Emilia was willing to risk everything in her determination to see Iain's debt satisfied and save their family name from the gossip mills.

"I will have you say it, Felix." Abner lifted his chin, but he noted the way his uncle's jaw trembled. "You care more for this slip of a woman than your blooded uncle."

"I do, and I will not make any apologies for it." Felix stared down his nose at his uncle, realizing the stark resemblance between them: their hair, their eyes, their height. Yet, that was where the similarities ended. Felix would never act the scoundrel and expect another to take on the burden of his troubles. He would never allow another to be in peril because of a hazardous decision that he made. Living in such a way was not the man Felix was, nor would he ever be. "Lady Emilia, and her siblings are everything my mother and father would have wished for me to find. They love fiercely. Their loyalty knows no bounds. And Lady Emilia has the strength of will I should have exhibited with you, Uncle."

Behind him, Felix heard the rustling of fabric. Had he spoken out of turn? Upset Emilia or her siblings?

But he knew with certainty that every word he'd spoken was true, and he'd never need take them back.

Felix longed to look over his shoulder, to reassure Emilia that he would never stop protecting her and her family against those who sought to cause them harm, including his own uncle.

And even with all he and Lady Emilia had been through over the last few days, she'd never depended on him, never given up and begged him to solve her family's troubles. She stood by his side while making the difficult decisions.

A shoulder brushed Felix's arm as Emilia stepped forward, slipping her hand into his as they faced Abner together. Everyone around them was forgotten: Lady Catriona, Lady Moire, and Lord Strathmore behind them, Harris before them, and Jameson in the distance. They all faded as Felix stood before Lord Abernathy.

The last of his kin.

The guardian who had been charged with caring for him after his father's death.

The man who should have taken charge of Felix and guided him into manhood.

Yet, before Felix stood the type of man Felix would live each day swearing not to become. While beside him was a woman he would be blessed to draw even an ounce of strength from. A woman with loyalty, tenacity, and love flowing through her veins as freely as the river Thames flowed unimpeded through London.

A small voice spoke behind him, "I think it best we continue this discussion in private, Your Grace."

Yes, Felix needed privacy, but not to continue his argument with his uncle.

He needed to speak with Lady Emilia, to tell her his longings for her and implore her to give him a chance after everything was settled with Harris.

CHAPTER 10

"REMAIN HERE, UNCLE," Felix commanded with a seriousness that Emilia could not fathom any man going against. "Harris, if you will wait here with Lord Abernathy, we will have everything settled—"

Emilia did not wait for Felix to finish but pivoted and stalked toward the abandoned stable yard. The horses remained on the field, their riders and grooms walking them leisurely around the track after their sprint.

Moire had been correct. What needed to be said should be discussed in private.

All of her best-laid plans were disintegrating before her very eyes.

She'd been a fool to think that winning a silly race would solve all her family's troubles. That repaying a debt would help her family remain in their current place on the fringes of society. And, most of all, that the secrets of their past would not find a way into their present.

They were not witches. It had been nearly one hundred years since the last woman, Janet Horne, was burned at the stake in Scotland. Witchcraft, spells, and sorcery were not practiced by her family and had never been a part of her legacy. But her gift was. And never had she used it with nefarious intentions.

Never had Moire applied her gift to hurt others.

Never would Catriona read the feelings of others only to cause them pain, for she would feel the agony as swiftly and as powerfully as they did.

Yet, society would soon know them for their past and their past alone.

But not even *their* past, that of their ancestors.

It would not take long for the hunters to come in search of Emilia, Catriona, and Moire, as well as their parents and Iain.

Emilia paced toward the far end of the stable stalls before turning and walking back toward her siblings, who waited closer to the track. Did they realize the danger they were in? Had they come to the same conclusion Emilia had?

They'd need to tell their father as soon as they returned to London. Preparations would need to be made, the house packed and readied to depart, and she would need to say goodbye to the home she'd come to love over the last several years.

Where would they go? Not back to Edinburgh. Her relations, though tied by blood, had no allegiance to anyone but themselves. Emilia could not blame them for recognizing that such a large group of Dalaises could not live unnoticed for long. They'd overstayed their welcome in Bath, too. Dalais Forge lay abandoned and rotting in Sunderland England...maybe she could convince her father they should return home.

Home. Such a foreign notion, an elusive place.

Not since their time in the root cellar at the Forge had Emilia felt at home. And even then, it had far more to do with who was with her than the place they congregated.

Her *seanmhair* and her siblings.

They were her home.

"Lady Emilia," the breathless whisper brought her to a halt as she stared straight ahead.

Felix stood before her as if conjured by some form of magic she did not possess. But, no, he'd likely followed so they could speak privately. The pained look in his brown eyes made the darkened splotches under them more apparent. The exhausted, burdened duke had returned, and Emilia couldn't help but think it was her doing.

He had been by her side, standing up to his uncle, yet how long could she expect him to continue down such a path. Lord Abernathy was his blood, his uncle, his only relation. No matter how angry Iain made her, she'd never fully turn her back on him, never shut him out of her life. How could she expect Felix to go to such lengths with Abernathy?

He'd made a choice in the moment he'd surely regret with time.

"Your Grace." She held up her hand to stop him from speaking further. Emilia knew the consequences of Iain's actions and her failed plan. "I understand, far more than others, that you must do what is best for your family and your future...just as I will do the same for mine. I will not fault you for that choice. There are things we cannot alter in our fate. This is one of them. While I hope you can convince your uncle to show my family mercy and keep our confidence, I understand that complete control over him is not within your power. With me and Iain, it is the same."

Emilia took a deep breath, imploring her knees to hold strong and not buckle beneath her. At least not until she and her siblings were safely in their coach and racing back toward London. "I understand that my family is not your concern. Lord Abernathy is your relation, and I would never ask you to compromise that kinship for me and my siblings. However, if you can convince your uncle to—"

The words escaped her in that moment. What was she requesting of Felix, and why did she think she had any right to ask it?

With their win today, they could settle their debt with Harris and Abernathy.

At least that part of her problem could be sorted and satisfied.

She should feel blessed that they did not need fear financial ruin as well as personal prosecution.

Emilia glanced past Felix to her siblings, her heart swelling at the mere sight of her wayward family. Iain was bright with remorse, while Cat's aura hinted at a healthy measure of hopefulness mixed with confusion. Moire...she was always harder to read as there was no reckoning if the haze surrounding her was due to the present circumstances or something in the future.

Bringing her stare back to Felix, Emilia expected to see many things, not only in his aura but also in his cocoa brown eyes.

Yet, what stared back at her was nothing

she'd anticipated. Felix had every right to be angry at their situation, to be steadfast in protecting his family name, to be hesitant to assist Emilia and her siblings at the risk of his uncle.

Felix had no other option available to him but his uncle's well-being. Emilia knew well the need to compromise her desires to protect and care for her family. She'd never turn her back on Moire, Cat, and Iain; and neither could she conclude that Felix would choose her over his family.

Family was everything.

The duke hadn't said a word, not once attempting to halt her as she spoke. Now, everything—all the trials and tribulations to come for her family—disappeared. Before her, Felix stood with an unmistakable glow surrounding him.

She knew the color well.

It was the same when her father looked upon her mother.

It was the same as when her *seanmhair* had looked upon Emilia and her siblings.

Pale pink.

True love...

Unable to look away, the aura around Felix turned turquoise at the edges.

The transformation was startlingly apparent. The turquoise spread through it, yet did not overtake the pale pink; they worked in unison.

Love, and the releasing of past hardships to embrace a new life.

She'd known how much Felix loved Lord Abernathy. They were the only kin each other had left. Yet, the haze had even Emilia feeling the strong bond. Felix had lived his entire life caring for his uncle, and that would not change...at least not that day.

Knowing the unbreakable bond between her and her siblings, Emilia would never expect that connection to diminish or disappear.

Yet, Felix was letting something go, it was what the turquoise haze signified.

The duke was letting go of a burden that he'd kept close for many, many years, and preparing to embrace a new life.

Did he realize that his uncle would never change and accept that fact, reconciling his future with the ever-present need to care for Lord Abernathy? To love the earl, despite his shortcomings?

Emilia could fully understand the need to love family despite their flaws.

It was the same with her and Iain.

And Emilia would never turn away from her siblings. Never forsake them for another. Never give up protecting them from the past that haunted them at every turn.

Nevertheless, her heart ached at Felix's choice. He'd seemed the only man who understood her all-encompassing need to care for her family, to protect their secret, to go to any lengths to keep them safe.

Despite their time together and their kiss; the connection Emilia could not deny, which was made all the more apparent by Felix's mixing auras of pink and turquoise, she feared it was not enough. Would never *be* enough.

The Duke of Kintore would choose his uncle, the same as Emilia would always put her siblings before all else.

CHAPTER 11

THE WARM AFTERNOON breeze swept through the stable yard, taking hold of Emilia's short hair and pushing it in front of her sapphire eyes. Without thinking, Felix reached forward and tucked it behind her ear. It was such a natural gesture, and he had the overwhelming feeling he'd done it a hundred times before—and would do it another thousand times in the years to come.

Though her siblings waited a hundred feet away, it was as if he and she were utterly alone in the world. The sounds of horses on the track, grooms running to and fro from the stables, and the departing carriages in the field not far away did nothing to drown out his labored breathing or the beating in his chest.

Far too soon, she looked away. "Your uncle—"

"My uncle is a grown man who has

depended on his nephew for years. And that is, regrettably, my fault. I allowed Abner's self-absorbed nature to draw me into his world of deceit without care for my own future. Day in and day out, I've allowed him to hurt me, each time the wound more and more superficial. Not because each was not grave, but because my sense of family, commitment, and love were tainted by my uncle's selfishness to the point where that signified our bond. He found trouble, and I proved my love for him by fixing what he broke." Felix brought his hands to cup her face, and she turned her nose to nuzzle the palm of his hand. "Being around you and your siblings has taught me that is not love. It is not what family should be about."

"Sometimes, it is about remedying problems," she whispered.

The sorrow in her tone had his heart skipping a beat. "Yes, yes, but...I do not know."

All words escaped him as his mouth was drawn to hers, imagining their lips pressed together, immediately transporting him back to their brief time locked in that room at the back of the pub. He paused, an almost immeasurable space separating their faces. It was a kiss he had no right to long for, though he sensed it was the only thing that would make him whole.

"The last several days with you, Lady Catriona, Lady Moire, and even Strathmore have been more enjoyable than all the years since my father's death." He hadn't meant to confess such a thing, as if her family woes were his entertainment. That wasn't what he'd meant to impart at all. "I thought I knew commitment, loyalty, and the bond that comes with it. However, the loyalty between my uncle and I has always been one-sided. I cannot continue to live in such a way."

Unfulfilled. Unappreciated. Unvalued. Unloved.

Emilia's hands covered his on her cheeks, squeezing gently as she held his stare. "I understand how you feel."

He wanted to demand to know how she, a woman so obviously loved and adored by all who knew her, could understand his anguish.

"I have seen it before, several times," she continued. "You will give everything for another, even your life. It has always been the way of things for my family. We sacrifice ourselves so that others can flourish until our life is nothing but giving up one thing after another after another. It never stops, and we never wish for it to because it is in that sacrifice that our life gains meaning."

Felix shook his head. He was done giving things up for a man who cared naught for him. If it were for someone he loved and who returned that affection, everything would be different. He would continue to give of himself until nothing was left.

Again, she did that thing where she looked at him and around him at the same time.

Though now he knew she was reading him—his emotions, his deepest feelings were laid bare before her, and he was helpless to hide anything from her.

Surprisingly, he had no urge to, no need to keep anything hidden from Emilia.

Unlike the hurt, disappointment, and betrayal he hid from his uncle each time he came to the older man's rescue.

"Life—and fate—are unpredictable and never what one hopes comes to pass." She sighed, her hands falling away from his as she took a step back. His hands cupped air where her face had been. "And so it will be for us. You must protect your family name and your uncle, and I cannot trust that Lord Abernathy will keep my family's gifts a secret. Thankfully, we are a nomadic group and will quickly find new lodging and a new place to consider home."

He noted her use of the word *consider*.

Not a new home, but a place to consider home.

"We shall move away from London and hope news does not follow us." A great sorrow filled her eyes, so much so that the sapphire hue clouded to mirror the murky depths of the sea. "I am indebted to you for all you've done for my siblings; however, it is time we recognize that my plan has failed."

Felix did not want to consider her departure from London. He could not begin to contemplate a future without her in it, even if they were not fated to be anything more than friends, mere acquaintances who greeted one another at societal functions.

Fated. Fate… Felix loathed the word.

He'd heard Emilia and her siblings use the term several times, and he could not get past the feeling that his fate, and that of Emilia's family, was not set in stone without the ability to alter the course, for that would signify his future was unchangeable. He was doomed to follow in his uncle's footsteps, fated to spend his life remedying the older man's troubles.

Fate, if it had a heart, would not want that for anyone.

How did he tell Emilia that he had no faith in fate?

The groan of wood planks beneath their feet sounded behind him, followed by the clearing of a throat.

"Mr. Harris," Emilia greeted the bookmaker with a nod.

"Lady Emilia." The man's tone was far lighter than it had been upon their first meeting, or even when Felix had come face-to-face with Harris to place his bet earlier that day. "I do hope I am not interrupting anything of import, but I have tasks to see to at the pub and wanted a word with you and Lord Strathmore before I depart."

Alarm etched Emilia's face. "Sorrel, our horse, won. You can keep our winnings to repay Iain's debt to you. It is satisfied, and you will never see us again. I promise."

Emilia's eyes pleaded for Felix to come to her aid. It was the first time she'd shown any need for his help, and bloody hell if he wouldn't be there for her. Though, once she heard what more Harris had to say, it wasn't aid she needed but an explanation.

Felix grinned before turning to face Harris, his hand held out for the bookmaker to grasp.

"Your Grace." The question in her tone was unmistakable as she moved to stand beside Felix. "What have you done?"

MOIRE TOOK IN her sister's bewilderment with a great measure of satisfaction and accomplishment. For the first time in their lives, Em was thinking of herself and her future before that of her family. It was as her *seanmhair* had wished for her eldest grandchild.

She hadn't longed for Emilia to put someone above her family, no…

Seanmhair Ailis had foreseen a day when the needs of their family and Emilia's fate would collide in perfect harmony. A man her granddaughter could love without the need to relinquish her family bond.

Because this lord and his loyalty to those he loved was so fierce and unending he'd fight every day to keep Emilia—and their entire family—safe. Much like a long-ago ancestor, Daniel Guaire, had done. A man of no blood bond who'd taken to saving and protecting what was left of the Dalais clan.

Thankfully, this time, their family was growing with untamed abandon, starting with the marriage and mating of Lady Emilia Noble to the Duke of Kintore.

Iain would be next to fall, followed three years later by Catriona.

She, well…Moire could not see her own fate, a problem she'd attempted to remedy time and time again to no avail.

Her *seanmhair* had clearly foreseen her own future; however, her granddaughter's gift was lacking in that regard.

For now, and all the days to come, Moire would find her pleasure in seeing the Dalais clan—the Noble family—flourish.

But first, the duke must prove that he and Em were fated to be.

She could not lead either her stubborn, steadfast sister nor the burdened but loyal duke to that final conclusion. No one could, not even their *seanmhair* had she still been of this earth.

Instead, Moire slipped her hand through Iain's to one side of her and grasped Cat's open palm on the other, and the trio started toward Emilia. An undeniable heat spread through them, connecting them and bonding them as one.

CHAPTER 12

SOMETHING WAS AMISS, and Emilia had utterly missed the indications, though they were now as clear as a Sunderland sunrise across the open meadows of her childhood home. An air of mischief mixed with Felix's yellow aura and told her that something was afoot even before she watched the duke extend his hand, and Harris reach forward to give it a vigorous shake.

It had only been two days prior when the bookmaker had accused them of assisting Iain and Lord Abernathy in skirting making good on their wagers and had subsequently locked them in that back room at the pub. Yet now, the men acted as friends?

Iain, with Cat and Moire in tow, came to stand close.

"Lord Strathmore," Felix waved Iain closer. "Harris requests a word."

When her brother moved away from Cat and

Moire, Emilia's stare settled on their youngest sister.

Her aura was far different than her siblings', as if she were already aware of what was transpiring and took great pleasure in Emilia being oblivious to it all.

Long-ago mutterings filled Emilia's mind. *"Moire, me wee darling, ye canna speak of that to ye sister. The future be what it is, with or without ye meddling..."*

A caution from her *seanmhair*, bestowed on Moire as Emilia had climbed up the ladder and out of the root cellar that final time at Dalais Forge. Their *seanmhair* had passed not long after that day, and Emilia and her siblings never entered the cellar again. In fact, they had quickly packed their belongings and moved on to Edinburgh.

If anything was clear and obvious, Moire had meddled.

Iain stood tall before the bookmaker, his shoulders thrown back, awaiting his judgement.

Harris held out a single note. "Your winnings, Lord Strathmore, after your debt at The Howling Owl was settled. You can cash the note in town or bring it back to London with you. But know your debts are settled, and your wagers are"—Harris nodded to Emilia before continuing—"no longer welcome in Epsom Downs."

The note hung in the air between Iain and Harris.

"I do not understand." Emilia stepped forward and took the note from Harris. "This was not what we discussed." The sum, handwritten on the cheque, was one hundred and twenty pounds. Their wager was supposed to repay both Iain's and Lord Abernathy's debts and nothing more. "This is too much, Mr. Harris. And why is this cheque only in my brother's name?"

She glanced at Felix, who had yet to say a word, but his continued grin told her he hadn't followed her plan.

"The wager placed today was made solely in Lord Strathmore's name. Therefore, his debt is paid, and I came to deliver his winnings personally," Harris said. "Ah, and here is Lord Abernathy."

The entire group turned to see Harris's henchman and another man dragging Abernathy's struggling form through the stable yard. The earl's polished boots attempted to gain purchase so he could pull free from his captors, but Emilia knew well the strength of Harris's men.

The cheque in her hand, endorsed by Epsom Holdings and Treasury, was for the exact amount Felix's uncle owed the bookmaker.

"Lord Abernathy." Harris issued a mock bow, his grand, sweeping gesture making his men chuckle as the earl pulled ever harder on the goons' hold. "I cannot think you mean to depart today without settling your various debts."

"Right sure he was," one of the men restraining Abernathy said. "Found him at his coach."

Harris advanced toward Abernathy, the bookmaker suddenly transformed into the man from The Howling Owl, menace in his glare. "Tsk-tsk. A lord who attempts to call off on settling his debts. What would your fancy friends think of such a cowardly action?"

Abernathy's stare darted around the gathering until they settled on his nephew.

Emilia couldn't help but pity Lord

Abernathy. From the looks on Cat's and Iain's faces, they also felt a measure of sympathy for him, as well.

"Felix," Abernathy pleaded, making one last futile pull on his trapped arms. "Tell him you will settle the debt, and I shall repay you...tenfold."

"I am done caring for you, Uncle." Felix clasped his hands behind his back, training his narrowed stare on Abernathy. "However, I will endeavor to do one last favor for you, but it will come at a steep price."

"Whatever you desire, my boy."

"I will pay off your debt to Harris, but you shall leave London...actually, all of England. Immediately. Journey to France or Scotland, it matters not to me. However, you will be gone. You will not speak of Lady Emilia or her family. You will never come to me again with your financial troubles."

"I cannot leave England," Abernathy sputtered. "I have friends, investments, responsibilities."

"You have an earldom that is in ruins, and debtors far and wide." Felix lifted his chin, and Emilia knew how difficult it was for him to give his only relation such an ultimatum. "I settle your account with Harris, and you leave England. Or...you remain, and so does your debt. Harris will spread word of your nefarious dealings, and I will do nothing to stop the gossip from spreading. I can only assume your friends will disappear, as will your invites from the *ton*, and your club membership will certainly be withdrawn. You will be ruined."

Abernathy let loose a strangled cackle. "If I am ruined, so will you be tainted, Felix. And we both know you have not cared for me all these years out of the goodness of your heart. You've done it to keep your name free from scandal."

Emilia longed for nothing more than to step forward and speak on Felix's behalf. He'd done everything for his uncle because he was searching every day for a love and kinship Abernathy was incapable of giving. He'd believed that if he settled one more debt, handled one more problem for the man, he would show his gratitude and love.

The dark red aura around Felix kept Emilia quiet.

Willpower, strength, and determination.

"I have spent my entire life loving you, Uncle. Just as you proport to have given up much to raise me, I have done without a lot to try and earn your love. But that time has come to an end. It was an endeavor I was never meant to accomplish. I know that now because of Lady Emilia and her family." A bit of Felix's resolve crumbled, and she stepped forward to take hold of his hand, praying her strength would transfer to him. "It is time I find my place—a family—based on love and mutual respect, not need and guilt."

In her heart, Emilia suspected that Felix could not, *would* not, follow through with his promise to allow ruin to touch his uncle.

As if reading her thoughts, Felix continued, "Those are your two options. Remaining in London and causing troubles for Emilia and her family is not one of them. But I can assure you, if you do not accept this kindness, your leisurely life will come to an abrupt end. It is in your best interest to go. You will make new friends wherever you settle, and I pray you make wise decisions with regards to your financial investments."

"Your choice, Lord Abernathy?" Harris crossed his arms. "I haven't all day."

Abernathy slumped between the two henchmen, his knees collapsed, and his head hung forward. "I will go. You've given me no other choice."

"Very wise," Felix mumbled.

"Release him," Harris commanded.

Abernathy slumped to the ground but was quickly pulled to his feet by Felix's driver.

"Jameson, escort my uncle to his townhouse. See to the packing of this things and ready him to depart on the morrow."

"Yes, Your Grace." The servant steered Abernathy away from the group.

Emilia squeezed Felix's hand once more as they both turned to watch Abernathy march toward the coach grounds.

"You did not have to do that, Felix." Emilia could not imagine banishing her brother from their family and their home; however, there was a big difference between Iain and Abernathy. "I do thank you for all you've done for my family."

"You are wrong." Felix turned toward her, taking hold of both her hands. "I *did* have to do exactly that because I cannot bear the thought of you moving away from London. And so, perhaps I am as selfish as my uncle. If the last few days have shown me anything, it is what I want for my life. It is not a future brimming with people who need me, but years surrounded by those who truly want me. In the same way you and your family's connection is based on so much more than dependency. It is about love."

Emilia stared up into Felix's tender, brown eyes. The toughest decision made in his life, and he had been thinking of her. He'd secured her family's safety and made certain his uncle said nothing of their secret, making it possible for the Noble family to remain in London.

Her sisters would have the opportunity to experience their debut Seasons, and Iain would one day take his place in parliament and secure himself as the heir to the Eglinton marquessate.

And Emilia...she'd be free to explore her connection with Felix, all without fear for her family.

She'd never thought to earn the love of such a worthy lord. Never in her wildest imaginings had she thought to follow in the path of her ancestors...

Once, a long time ago, and many more times throughout the generations, Dalais women had bonded themselves to men worthy of their family secret. Men who would sacrifice themselves to keep their legacy hidden. Men who loved their women fiercely and committed themselves fully. Men who risked it all for love.

Emilia had recognized all these traits in Felix the first time he appeared at her doorstep with a battered Iain in tow.

Trust had come naturally between them.

And, just as easily, his aura had shown his true feelings for her. Love.

Even if she'd misread it a time or two, fearing such a deep, intimate connection with anyone besides her family would never be hers...

CHAPTER 13

THE DAY HAD quickly waned. Felix had made the arrangements to settle Abner's debts with the bookmaker and gather Emilia and her siblings in preparation to depart Epsom. He'd attempted to send them on their way, knowing their extended absence from London would draw considerable notice from their father; nevertheless, she had declared that they would all leave together or not at all.

And, truthfully, Felix could think of nothing worse than standing helplessly by as Emilia's carriage pulled away from the racetrack with no guarantee of when he'd see her again. When he'd stare into her clear, sparkling, blue eyes, feel the need to run his hands through her hair, or pull her close for a kiss, their lips meeting as they had that day at The Howling Owl—as if they'd been made to meet.

With his obligations satisfied, he now sat

across from her in the Kintore coach, her maid having been banished to escort the rest of the Noble family on their journey back to London. Rosemary, Emilia's maid, had protested profusely; however, in the end, she'd done as her mistress commanded, and Felix was happy for the few hours alone with Emilia that the drive afforded.

There was so much more he wanted to tell her, yet no definitive place to begin.

In the end, she'd been the one to speak first while he'd spent the quiet minutes taking in her splendor, from her unfashionably cropped hair to her wide, round, blue eyes and heart-shaped lips. Much of their short time together had been steeped in urgency, either at The Howling Owl or the track. Even their first moments together, it had been Iain who'd taken center stage.

"How did you know he'd choose to leave England?" Her question was emotionally charged, yet little more than a whisper. Her hands wrung in her lap, but her gaze was steadily fastened on his.

It wasn't the first query he'd thought she'd pose; however, Felix needed but a moment to reply. "Unlike myself—and you—my uncle is always one to put himself and his comforts before all else." Felix reached across the space, settling his hand on her fidgeting fingers and bringing her full attention to him. Though her hands stopped moving, she nibbled on her bottom lip as her anxiety continued. Felix would do his utmost to banish her worry. "Once he was aware of his fate if he remained in England, Abner's path was clear. The things he cared about most—possessions, the opinions of society, his fine dress, and the appearance of wealth— were all stripped away, and nothing was left of him—or *for* him in London. Despite his title as my guardian in my youth, he was never present for me."

"I cannot imagine giving him an ultimatum was easy." She sighed, her eyes pooling with sympathetic tears. "He is your uncle."

"And I am his nephew," Felix countered. "But blood means nothing without love. Just as a connection based on love has come to mean everything. That is what I've found."

Felix was pleased that she took a moment to read his aura. She'd taught him so much, the most important being that one could not hide their true emotion of the moment. Not from her. And Felix didn't desire that at all. He wanted Emilia to know with certainty that all he said, and all he felt, was true without hesitation.

Given freely and completely.

Her shoulders tensed as confusion drew her brow low over her shining, blue eyes before understanding sank in. "I thought those deep feelings, the shifting of your aura, was for another...your uncle, perhaps."

His smile was wide enough to foretell what his heart knew to be true. "Between societal ruin and a forced holiday, the choice was simple for Abner. Mayhap the time away will change him, make him a better man. But, regardless, I could not have him remaining in England and jeopardizing your family's safety. And if you departed town, so would I follow. As my uncle's decision was evident, mine was as simply made."

"But with Lord Abernathy gone, my family is protected."

"Yes, but one never knows what tomorrow will bring, and I intend to be close—as close as you'll allow—to make certain you and your family remained protected." Felix wanted Emilia close for more than what he could provide her. He wanted her for what she could give him.

A sense of home.

Family.

Connection.

Unbreakable bonds.

Love.

An enduring legacy that he would strive every day to ensure.

Her story was rooted in the past, yet Felix suspected his story had only just begun.

His purpose in life had finally been recognized.

"I wish to have you close every day." She leaned forward until no space separated them across the carriage. Her breath caressed his cheek, and the aroma of her, flowery with a hint of dust from the track, enveloped him. "My *seanmhair* was adamant about trusting only those you love and loving only those worthy of trust. Without that conscious thought taking up ample room in our minds, my family would have fallen to the hunters nearly two hundred years ago. However, my ancestors lived by this way of life."

She paused, and Felix feared she'd pull away from him.

"I've lived my life as my grandmother taught. My siblings and I, we love and trust one another implicitly. Certainly, Iain has his times of bad decisions, but he would protect Moire, Cat, and I until the end. My father, as well." Emilia's stare narrowed on his as if she were waging some internal war, making a decision she hoped wasn't foolhardy. "There are men—and women, such as my mother—who have kept the Dalais family secret. Some have protected it with their lives. I have no doubt that you, Felix, are one of those people. I saw it that first day, and you've proven it true each day after. It was as if fate brought you to my doorstep and challenged me to turn you away, to not see the gift that had been bestowed upon me."

Did Emilia not realize it had been the same for him?

His entire existence since his father's passing had been focused on saving Abner from his vile ways and himself. There had been no shining light at the end of the tunnel for Felix, no long-awaited day when everything would change, and he'd be able to live life according to his own wants and needs. First and foremost, his daily life revolved around his uncle.

But no more.

"Perhaps it was I who was fated to find you," Felix countered, the truth of his words burrowing deep. "You were meant to set me free, to show me what my future could hold if I let go of the past and embraced..." Did he dare be so bold? "You."

"I believe my *seanmhair* saw you in my future, knew my fate years before my existence." Emilia placed a soft kiss on his parted lips; a meeting that sent a shiver through him before she pulled away again.

All this talk of fate and futures and those knowing what was to come for them should have made Felix uneasy, yet it was a sense of rightness...of surety...that coursed through him.

"If your grandmother predicted our match, who are we to fight fate?"

"Are you saying I am fated for the duke?" she said with a light laugh.

"Fate. The word held no meaning for me only a fortnight ago. In fact, I downright disliked it. But now..." He paused, pressing his lips to hers, eliciting a sigh that had him longing to reach out and bring her across the carriage and onto his lap. Felix knew if he did that, their discussion would come to an end because he would be unable to keep his mouth from hers, his hands from her body, and his thoughts in any logical order. And so, just as she had done, he pulled away. "Now...now I desperately long for something such as fate to be true. However, it will never dictate my feelings for you. Even if it dragged us apart, I would return to you time and time again. Because I love you, Emilia."

There was no surprise in her eyes, no hesitation before she spoke, and no quiver in her tone. "That is very good to hear because I love you, as well. I am not certain when it happened or how it evaded my notice for so long, but my heart is fated to yours. Your future and mine are intertwined. I trusted you the moment you returned Iain to our family. Mayhap my fondness and affection began in that moment. Or our time in that room at The Howling Owl. One cannot be certain." She shrugged. "Though I suspect that is not important. Only that it is unequivocally true and all-encompassing."

EPILOGUE

Sunderland, England
April 1812

MOIRE, WITH CAT and Iain by her side, watched as Felix—yes, the entire family addressed the duke by his given name now as he was one of their own—climbed down the rickety ladder into the root cellar at Dalais Forge. Felix had been unyielding in his resolve to test the thing before any of the Noble siblings— especially his betrothed, Emilia—descended the ancient, wooden thing and risked injury if the ladder broke a rung or collapsed altogether.

Peering down into the darkened depths, Moire smiled when Felix placed his hand on Em's ankle, then her leg, her back, and finally took her hand as she stepped off the ladder to safety on the cellar floor. His gaze traveled the length of Emilia's body as he assessed that she was, indeed, whole and unharmed by the climb down.

It was a journey they'd made often in their youth; however, things had changed dramatically in the ten years since they'd gathered at their ancestral estate. The gardens were overgrown, the bedchambers abandoned and outdated yet clean, and the roof was in desperate need of repairs.

To Moire's chagrin, the root cellar hadn't changed at all...not even the dank aroma of rot that was startlingly familiar and oddly comforting.

Felix's smiling face came into view again as he held his hand upward. "Who is next?"

Catriona hesitantly stepped forward and scurried down the ladder, followed by Iain, and finally, Moire.

Once below, Moire marveled at how small and cramped the space felt with all five of them gathered, though it was no more crowded than their carriage ride to Dalais Forge had been with all of them crammed into Felix's traveling coach. Moire's parents, the Marquess and Marchioness of Eglinton, followed closely behind for their three days of travel. Yet, a third coach trailed at a more leisurely pace, to transport her family's trunks and several servants.

"Catriona, do ye ken why we be down here?" Moire intoned, using her *seanmhair's* Scottish brogue.

Iain chuckled while Felix glanced at Em and whispered something in her ear. Emilia shielded her smile and whispered back to her betrothed, the sparkle in her eyes visible even in the dim cellar light.

Catriona, always happy to play along, squared her shoulders and lifted her chin before speaking, her sapphire eyes mirroring Em's.

When Moire turned her hardened glare on Cat, they all giggled.

"We mustn't ever put from mind that we are all special. Our gifts, blessed unto us by our Dalais ancestors, are of great privilege and should not be used for evil. We are descendants of a trio of powerful siblings—Niall, Sorcha, and Caitriona—who gave up their lives to bring each of us into this world." She paused, meeting each of their identical stares before settling on the newcomer among them. "We are to trust in our gifts. We are to trust in one another. And, above all else, we are to be leery of any person not of Dalais blood."

The time had come, and Moire reached into the pocket of her white apron to retrieve the sealed note left to her by their *seanmhair*. For years, she'd anguished over telling her siblings of its existence and opening the note, reading it alone, and burning it immediately.

In the end, she'd kept the note closed at all times but never allowed herself to ponder it, as Em would have spotted her deceptive aura, and Cat would have sensed her torment.

On the outside, in *Seanmhair's* jarring print made nearly illegible as her mangled hands had grown nearly unusable in her final months, were printed the nine simple words Moire had read nearly a thousand times: *Ye shall know when to read, me wee lass.*

Witnessing the ever-increasing love blossom so wholly around Felix and Emilia that it encompassed the entire Noble family had led Moire to realize that this was the moment her *seanmhair* had hinted at. The moment she'd seen in her visions all those years ago. The same instant she'd attempted to convey in hushed whispers to her *seanmhair* that day in this very cellar.

The time to read the letter was now.

With Iain, Cat, Emilia—and Felix—as witnesses.

Moire stared down at the note clutched tightly in her hands. If she opened it, her last and final connection to her *seanmhair* would be gone. It was as if she and the older woman had kept a magical secret between the pair of them all these years, and now it was to be exposed—the magic gone.

"What have you there?" Felix asked.

Moire raised her eyes to the duke's, her legacy mark growing warm on her ankle.

It was odd, but she'd never given the triangle birthmark much thought until the day at Epsom Downs when it had lit with heat—not uncomfortable but unfamiliar. She noted that Cat had gently touched the spot just above her left elbow, while Emilia massaged her hip. Even Iain seemed to be affected as he placed his open palm on his chest.

"Has it grown uncomfortably warm all of a sudden?" Felix pushed up the sleeves of his shirt to reveal his bare arms, a light dusting of dark hair covering his skin. "Perhaps I should return upstairs and lie down for a spot of rest."

Emilia's questioning stare met Cat's, and the pair shrugged, as confused as Felix.

If she'd desired any further proof that today was the day her *seanmhair* had written of, it stood before her.

Or, more aptly put, *he* stood among *them.*

He belonged with them.

He had been chosen, likely before his birth, just as Moire and her siblings had been bestowed with their gifts.

Moire had discovered that long-ago December day in the root cellar of Dalais Forge that Emilia was fated for the duke...but it had taken nearly ten years for the Duke of Kintore to enter their lives—and give Emilia the love she deserved.

The love that had become so evident between the pair that even the burdens that had weighed upon Felix for all his life had disappeared. He laughed, he loved, and he lived—with Emilia's happiness first and foremost in his mind.

"Please, do not go," Moire said. "I have something to show you all. From *Seanmhair*. She penned it for this very day."

She slipped her glove from her hand, tucking it into the pocket of her apron, and broke the seal on the note.

Unfolding the paper, Moire sensed four pairs of eyes trained on her as she smoothed the letter and held it aloft.

Scrawled across the top read: *Felix Huntar, the Duke of Kintore.*

"I believe she meant for you to read this." Moire handed the note to Felix. His shoulders tensed, and his brow drew low in question. "Go on."

"There must be a mistake," he countered.

"*Seanmhair* never made mistakes," Cat chimed in.

Felix didn't move but glanced at Emilia, who nodded for him to take the note. His hand trembled as he took hold of the paper, but his stare remained trained on Emilia. It was as if the pair had an entire conversation without speaking a word.

"Mother will be calling us shortly for supper," Iain said, breaking the silent connection between Em and Felix. "Do hurry up and get on with it. As most things to do with our family's past, whatever the missive holds will not include me, the ungifted Noble heir."

"Go on, Felix," Cat prodded. "Have a read."

Moire glanced around the cellar to see each of her siblings give the duke an encouraging smile. They'd all been touched by *Seanmhair* Ailis's gift during their years. All of them but Felix. It would be yet another connection forged between them. A shared bond that would last a lifetime.

Felix cleared his throat at the same time that Em, Cat, and Iain pushed closer.

Moire had no need to see her grandmother's sprawling script. The words had been ingrained in her mind for many, many years.

> *My* m'eudail. *Duke of Kintore, Felix Huntar.*
> *You have been sent to care for me wee ones. I knew ye*
> *before ye knew yourself. Ye are kind with a fierce*
> *loyalty me kin deserves. You have been given a gift—a*
> *verra special gift—the love of me brave lass, Emilia.*
> *Treasure it, and her. Always.*

"Children?" Moire glanced up the ladder to see her mother's head peek over the ledge. "What in heaven's name are you doing down there?"

"Nothing."

Moire couldn't help but smile when the siblings' voices rang out in unison.

"Do come up here now," her mother scolded. "Cook will be devastated if her duck soup grows cold before the lot of you are at the table."

"We will be up in but a moment, Mother," Em called, turning her focus back to her betrothed. "What does it say?"

"We dare not anger Cook," Moire said, catching Felix's eye. "Certainly, the letter can wait for another time. It has remained unread for this long already."

If you would like to know what the rest of the letter foretells for the Noble family, including what *Seanmhair* and Moire saw for their future, watch for Iain's story, THE UNGIFTED NOBLE HEIR, coming late 2019!

Author's Notes

Thank you for reading *Fated For The Duke!* If you enjoyed *Fated For The Duke,* be sure to write a brief review at any retailer.

I'd love to hear from you!
You can contact me at:
Christina@christinamcknight.com
Or write me at:
P.O. Box 1017
Patterson, CA 95363

www.ChristinaMcKnight.com
Check out my website for giveaways, book reviews, and information on my upcoming projects, or connect with me through social media at:
Twitter: @CMcKnightWriter
Facebook:
www.facebook.com/christinamcknightwriter
Goodreads:
www.goodreads.com/ChristinaMcKnight

Sign up for my newsletter here:
http://hyperurl.co/CMNL

Turn the page for an excerpt from
Bound by the Christmastide Moon,
where two strangers find love under the glowing moon of the Cornwall shore!

AN EXCERPT FROM
BOUND BY THE CHRISTMASTIDE MOON

Ditchley Hall, Southampton, England
June 1811

SILAS ANSON, THE eighth Earl of Lichfield, glared across the vast, disorderly expanse of what he'd recently come to view as *his* desk, not the unfamiliar, cluttered stretch of flat surface that had once belonged to his father.

A man he barely remembered and could not conjure in his mind.

On the receiving end of Silas's scowl was none other than Mr. Horace Peabody, Esquire.

The solicitor had also come with the Lichfield title and estate.

Though Silas silently debated which was of lesser value to him: his non-existent heritance or his father's trusted advisor.

"You are telling me—" Silas clamped his mouth shut, pondering and discarding his next statement as overly crass and unwarranted, no matter the validity of it. "You are telling me I was summoned back to England, ripped from my home in France, to inherit a title and estate so entrenched in debt that ruination can only be staved off for a month's time?"

Mr. Peabody, who surprisingly in no way resembled a pea of any sort, stared mutely at Silas from behind his rounded spectacles, his hands clenched on the stack of folders in his lap. Did the man realize how cliché he appeared? Glasses, ink-stained fingers, nerves so frazzled he shook, and the piles of paperwork. Lord above, the man had arrived with an entire forest's worth of the stuff. One could only imagine the mines exploited to collect the graphite needed to scribble all the nonsense that'd been presented to Silas.

And the solicitor had appeared anxious since his arrival.

"This plan you've so graciously detailed for me is the only viable option you have been able to ascertain for rescuing the Lichfield name?" Silas needed to hear Peabody verbalize his recommended course one last time; but the solicitor only nodded, his glasses slipping down the bridge of his nose. Silas wondered if he shouldn't seek other counsel in this matter—and every matter to come. "My estate is bankrupt, the title worthless, and my only recourse—if I refuse to throw myself at the mercy of my mother's family—is as outlined on this single sheet of paper?"

To further punctuate the absurdity of the situation, Silas retrieved the aforementioned document with its hastily written paragraph and held it high for Peabody to inspect.

"That is, indeed, my recommendation, my lord," Peabody croaked, bowing his head.

If his father were not solidly in his grave, Silas would do away with the previous earl himself.

Bloody damnation, but Silas—along with his mother and siblings—had been content and otherwise entertained in Paris all these years. That was before he'd been unceremoniously summoned back to his father's homeland to usurp a title he'd never thought to possess.

Silas slumped in his seat and scrubbed his face, attempting to gain some clarity on the situation—yet, it eluded him still.

His mother, Mary Louisa Anson, Lady Lichfield, had absconded from England over fifteen years prior, her three young children in tow, never to see her husband again. Edmond Anson hadn't come looking for his family, hadn't sent so much as a messenger to check on their whereabouts or safety, nor the authorities to return his offspring to their rightful place in England.

As the years passed and no one came for them, Silas and his siblings adjusted to life in France as their mother pursued her passion for art. He'd assumed his father had forged a new life and continued as if his twin sons and young daughter had never existed.

The solicitor perked up, a new spark of hope

lighting his otherwise lackluster stare. "You can always reach out to Mrs. Hambly. I have heard she is a fair woman who loves her relations. Do not so readily cast her—and your other aunts—aside. Perhaps the Countess of Somerton will be willing to step in and assist—"

Silas snorted. Yes, he'd been regaled with tales of the formidable Regina, his mother's sister, for years, and none of them spoke to her fair nature or love for her family, but rather to her need to be in control. "If my aunt cared a whit for her *relations,* she would have pursued my mother and offered assistance. Yet, my siblings and I lived on little more but stale bread and broth for years, residing above a butcher's shop in an unsavory part of Paris." Silas would not go into detail about the horrid conditions of his childhood—not with this man, at least. "No, that is not an option, at least not at this juncture."

"My plan will only solve a fraction of your problems, my lord." Peabody sighed, glancing toward the closed door of the study, his wide stare begging for any interruption as a means for escape. "And the solution itself is only temporary, at best."

"How could my father allow his estate to fall into such shambles?" Silas mused, expecting no answer, for any retort would not satisfy him.

"Because he was heartbro—" The solicitor's words cut short, and he swallowed. The tall clock chimed four times, echoing through the cavernous corridors of Ditchley Hall. "If there is nothing else you require, I will see myself out and prepare to depart for London."

Peabody stood, his lean, lanky body spoke of a man trapped behind a desk in a moldy room for over half his day, his pale skin in desperate need of sunlight.

Silas wanted the man gone, out of his office and away from Ditchley altogether. Away before word traveled to his siblings about the dire state of their affairs. Yet, that would not improve his family's situation nor hold the creditors at bay for long.

"Sit." His command reverberated off the walls and shook the windowpanes, sending a shiver down his spine. That was one positive of Ditchley Hall: his voice was a fearsome sound in every room. "I wish to speak further about my course for the next several months if I entertain your plan."

Regaining his seat, the solicitor shuffled through his folders in search of something, likely the means to keep Silas's wrath at bay a bit longer.

"An arranged marriage…"

"Yes, Lord Lichfield," Peabody nodded. "My notion to rescue the estate—at least for the time being—and keep your name and that of your siblings from the gossip mills, is to secure a mutually beneficial match."

"Mutually beneficial?" Silas had never envisioned himself wedded, especially after his parents' disastrous match. The only ones to suffer were the children of Edmond and Mary Louisa Anson. "What have I to offer a woman with a healthy enough dowry to sustain Ditchley Hall and provide for my siblings' immediate futures?"

Silas was speaking in questions once again, yet, when a man had no answers of consequence, all that was left was questions.

His entire life since fleeing England had been about finding answers…solutions to the many looming problems that plagued his family. When his mother had embraced her creative ways once across the Channel and neglected her children's upbringing, it had been up to Silas to find the means to educate his siblings, Slade and Svbil. He'd spent countless hours at the *Bibliothèque nationale de France*, first teaching himself to read, and then returning to their meager flat with the tomes necessary to instruct his brother and sister.

"You have a generations-old—and might I add, respected—title with connections to far more powerful members of society." Peabody recited the line as if he'd practiced it the entire journey from London. "That being said, I do not think it wise, or advantageous in your precarious position, to speak of the strained ties between you and your most notable relations."

Silas fairly growled. "Do you think me foolish enough to begin every conversation with the scandalous details of my mother's banishment?"

The solicitor's gaze swung back to Silas, his brow furrowed. "Your mother—errr, Lady Lichfield—was not banished. Has never been spoken of in anything but the highest regard by my employer, I mean to say, the previous Lord Lichfield...your father." Peabody held up a single finger as he riffled through his papers once more. "Ah, yes, here it is. Your father commissioned this letter in the event that your mother returned to England after his death. It states that in accordance with British law, she is, always has been, and will remain, Lady Lichfield. While you are the Lichfield heir, your mother is entitled to a hefty allowance and an estate, if she so chooses to accept it."

Chooses to accept it.

Most peculiar phrasing, indeed.

"I'm assuming this has the stipulation that it is only enforceable after my father's death." The statement drew another uneasy glance from the solicitor, and bloody hell if Silas wasn't remorseful over his lack of enthusiasm to review the piles of paperwork littering his desk. "Because there is no other reason *my father* would have allowed his *family* to live in squalor in Paris if there were funds and property set aside for my mother."

The solicitor once again focused on the folder before him, flipping pages until he found what he searched for. He lowered his head further, his lips moving as he read. "There is no such clause, my lord."

"Then why—" Silas stopped himself once more, knowing his fury would find no peace by harming the messenger. There was little use demanding to understand the inner workings of his late father. "Let us return to your original plan."

"Very good, my lord." The man's head bobbed up and down, obviously aware he'd avoided Silas's displeasure for the time being. "I have it all written down before you."

"Yes, however, there seems to be one crucial flaw."

"Oh?" the solicitor asked, leaning forward over his stack of papers to see the page on Silas's desk. "What would that be?"

Silas snatched the document and held it before him. "It details my need to wed—and marry for a healthy dowry—however, it does not purport *whom*, precisely, I should espouse." When the solicitor remained silent, he continued. "Being new to society, you should be well *aware* I am blissfully *unaware* of whom, exactly, has a sizeable dowry—and who will only bring increased hardship to the Lichfield name."

"I would never seek to command you in

whom to wed, my lord."

Odd, as the man had sent numerous correspondences about what was needed to keep the earldom afloat for another quarter.

Silas massaged his temples as he eyed the solicitor.

Would anyone truly miss the incompetent man if he were not to make it back to London?

Yet, he must needs remember he was in England once more, not the uncivilized country of France—as most Englishmen were fond to classify those who chose to live across the Channel.

"By chance have you any *suggestions* for proper, financially well-endowed ladies I should seek to court?"

Peabody broke into a broad smile as if Silas had finally asked the exact question he'd been waiting to hear. "I happen to have a client who..."

"How very fortunate..."

"Yes, well, he is not actively seeking a marriage for his daughter but has sought my advice on several occasions in regards to finding a match for her."

"Her worth?"

"Pardon?" Peabody said with a gulp.

"What is her worth? If I am to sell myself to the highest bidder, I would know the reward is sufficient to see me through for several years." Silas would never entertain a union unless he reaped adequate benefits: funds enough to see his siblings accepted into society, and prestige to overshadow his mother's estranged family. "Also, I suppose I should hear what you know of the girl."

"Her dowry is sufficient if you adhere to my other advice on managing your estate and investing in appropriately modest ventures. The woman in question is the only daughter of a marquess—a wealthy and connected marquess. If you have aspirations for the House of Lords, he will be an admirable advocate."

"I have never seen myself as a political man."

"Then, perhaps, you will be more in line with her brother. He is an earl and quite the man about town. A confirmed rakehell with an untouchable reputation in business, and a propensity for the gaming tables."

This earl seemed more suited as a friend for Slade, as opposed to an ally for Silas. "I would have the family name."

"The Marquess and Marchioness of Blandford." The solicitor again searched his paper, his finger running down the page until he found what he sought. "Their daughter, aged eighteen summers, is Lady Mallory Hughes."

Silas only hoped the woman did not have a third eye—or worse, the facial hair of a man. Silas supposed the son of a flighty countess could not expect much on his return to England, and the advantages of the match certainly outweighed the negatives. He needed money and means to see him and his siblings settled among the *ton*. Things that his father hadn't seen fit to provide.

"You will handle the paperwork?" Silas inquired, his brow rising in challenge.

"Without a doubt, my lord." Peabody pushed to his feet again, clutching his folders to his narrow chest as the stack threatened to escape and cascade to the floor. "I will write him at once upon my return to London. I am certain he will entertain the match."

Silas remained seated as Peabody scurried

from the room. Odd a man of such height and thin frame could scurry, but that he did. With any luck, the solicitor would arrive in London and secure the proper paperwork within a fortnight.

The grandfather clock chimed once more—five loud gongs, echoing through the house, reminding Silas he was to meet his siblings in the grand hall for supper.

ABOUT THE AUTHOR

USA TODAY Bestselling Author Christina McKnight writes emotional and intricate Regency Romance with strong women and maverick heroes.

Her books combine romance and mystery, exploring themes of redemption and forgiveness. When she's not writing, Christina enjoys trying new coffeehouses, visiting wine bars, traveling the world, and watching television.

Email: Christina@ChristinaMcKnight.com
Follow her on Twitter: @CMcKnightWriter
Keep up to date on her releases:
www.christinamcknight.com
Like Christina's FB Author page:
ChristinaMcKnightWriter

www.ingramcontent.com/pod-product-compliance
Lightning Source LLC
Chambersburg PA
CBHW021053130626
46552CB00005B/2074